SEVEN DEADLY SINS

Wrath

ROBIN WASSERMAN

SIMON PULSE
New York  London  Toronto  Sydney

This book is a work of fiction. Any references to historical events, real people, or real locales are used fictitiously. Other names, characters, places, and incidents are the product of the author's imagination, and any resemblance to actual events or locales or persons, living or dead, is entirely coincidental.

SIMON PULSE
An imprint of Simon & Schuster Children's Publishing Division
1230 Avenue of the Americas, New York, NY 10020
Copyright © 2006 by Robin Wasserman
All rights reserved, including the right of reproduction in whole or in part in any form.
SIMON PULSE and colophon are registered trademarks of Simon & Schuster, Inc.
Designed by Ann Zeak
The text of this book was set in Bembo.
Manufactured in the United States of America
First Simon Pulse edition July 2006
10  9  8  7  6  5  4  3  2  1
Library of Congress Control Number 2005933859
ISBN-13: 978-0-689-87785-8
ISBN-10: 0-689-87785-4

# Hell hath no fury . . .

*I feel nothing,* Beth thought, watching the tiny red light flash on her phone. *I see his name flash up on the screen, again and again, and I feel . . . nothing.*

It was just after dawn and she was at work. These days she was always at work, she thought bitterly, plunging the first batch of fries into the deep fryer and switching on the coffeemaker.

The phone rang a third time and, without warning, the wave of rage swept over her. It beat against her, pummeling her with the whys she couldn't answer. *Why me?*

She pictured Adam rolling around in bed with Kaia, while they were still together. She pictured Kane and his lying smile, touching her, stealing her trust. She pictured Harper whispering poisonous nothings in Jack Powell's ear. It wasn't fair, she raged.

And when another part of her responded: *Life isn't fair,* it only fueled her anger.

Beth began refilling the ketchup jars, wiping off the lids. And she instructed herself to calm down.

Maybe deep breaths.

Counting to ten . . . or a hundred.

It all might have worked—but instead, she tightened her grip on the ketchup bottle, and then, without thinking, flung it across the room. It shattered against the wall, spraying glass through the air and leaving a garish smear of red dripping down the stained tile.

Beth should have felt horrified or panicked, afraid of herself—or for herself.

But she didn't.

She felt better.

# SEVEN DEADLY SINS

*Lust*
*Envy*
*Pride*
*Wrath*

**SOON TO BE COMMITTED:**
*Sloth*

For Michelle Nagler and Bethany Buck,
extraordinary editors who have given me
an extraordinary opportunity

. . . let grief convert to anger; blunt not the heart, enrage it.
　　　　　—William Shakespeare, *Macbeth*

And all I really want is some patience
A way to calm the angry voice
And all I really want is deliverance.
—Alanis Morissette, "All I Really Want"

# preface

It was a mistake.

It had to be.

She'd heard wrong. Or it was a lie.

A dream. A nightmare. Something.

Because if it was true—

If it was true, and this was reality, there was no going back to the person she'd been. Before.

She remembered that person. Hard. Angry. Fury coursing through her veins. It had consumed her, until her focus narrowed to a single point, a single goal: vengeance.

It had been the perfect plan, every detail seamlessly falling into place. She had lain awake imagining how it would play out—wondering whether it would still the howling voice inside her, not that she'd finally given in to what it most desired.

Vengeance.

The plan had worked. Everything had unfolded as she'd imagined it. She'd gotten exactly what she'd wanted. But . . .

*She'd made a mistake. A fatal error. Because it hadn't gone* exactly *as planned, had it?*

*There was supposed to be humiliation—and there was.*

*There was supposed to be suffering—and there was.*

*Everything had gone the way it was supposed to. Except—*

*No one was supposed to die.*

Two weeks earlier . . .

# chapter

## 1

Harper burrowed deeper beneath the covers. How was she supposed to sleep with all that banging?

"Come on, Grace, open up."

Damn her parents. Which part of "I don't want to see anyone" did they not understand?

"We're bored," Kaia complained through the door.

"Come out and play with us!" Kane added, in that little-boy voice most girls found irresistible.

Harper Grace wasn't most girls.

"Go away," she shouted, her voice muffled by the pillow pressed over her head. "Please!"

With that, the door opened—and the covers flew off the bed.

"Time's up, Grace," Kane said, flinging away the comforter. "No more feeling sorry for yourself."

"Screw you. I could have been naked under here!" Harper said indignantly, suddenly realizing that the ratty sweatpants and faded gray Lakers T-shirt was an even more embarrassing ensemble.

"Why else do you think I did it?" Kane asked, chuckling.

How could he laugh?

The three of them had worked so hard to split up Beth and Adam and, for an all too brief moment, they'd finally gotten everything they'd wanted. Kane got Beth. Harper got Adam. And Kaia . . . got to stir up some trouble, which seemed to be all she needed. But now? Everything had come to light, and gone to shit. They were alone. How could Kane laugh, when Harper could barely stand?

"What are *you* looking at?" Harper snapped at Kaia as she climbed out of bed and wrapped a faux silk robe around herself. She hated the idea of Kaia seeing her bedroom, all the shoddy, mismatched furniture and cheap throw pillows; compared with Kaia's surely elegant and unbearably expensive digs, it probably looked like the pathetic "before" shot on one of those lame home-makeover shows.

Harper sighed. Even the prospect of trading insults with her former rival didn't deliver the jolt of energy it should have—not now that Kaia was one of only two friends that Harper had left. Some friends.

*A heartless playboy. A soulless bitch. And me,* Harper thought sourly.

Not quite the Three Musketeers.

"We're here to cheer you up," Kane said. "So cheer."

"Like it's that easy," Harper grumbled. Though, obviously, it had been for him.

"We even brought reinforcements," he added, pulling a

bottle of Absolut from his pocket with a magician-like flourish.

"What, is that your answer to everything?" Harper asked harshly. "If you hadn't been so drunk last week, and opened your big mouth—"

"Children, children," Kaia cut in, placing a perfectly manicured hand on Kane's broad shoulder. "I thought we agreed we were going to move past all that unpleasantness, kiss and make up. Her voice was soft and light, with a razor's edge—that was Kaia. Beautiful and dangerous.

As if Harper was scared of her.

"I don't care what we agreed," she shot back. "If Kane hadn't opened his big, stupid mouth . . . if Beth and Adam hadn't overheard his stupid bragging . . ." She couldn't finish.

"And if I hadn't opened *my* big, stupid mouth, the two lovebirds would be back together right now instead of at each other's throats," Kaia reminded her. "But no need to thank me, and no need to blame him. Even if he's an idiot."

"Hey!" Kane protested. But he was smiling—the infamous Kane smirk, which not even heartbreak could wipe off his face.

"Thanks for the pick-me-up, guys," Harper said, "but I'm not interested. You're dismissed."

"Are you just going to wallow here forever?" Kane asked in disgust. "Doesn't sound like the Grace I know and love."

"As if," she snorted. "I *meant,* I've got better things to do than play guest of honor at your little pity party."

"Like what?" Kaia asked skeptically.

"Like getting ready for my date," Harper lied. She

rolled her eyes. "Did you really think I was going to spend Saturday night in bed? Or at least, in *my* bed? Please." She shook her head as if pitying their poor reasoning skills. "I'm just resting up for the main event."

"Now that's more like it," Kane said, his smirk widening into a grin. Kaia just narrowed her eyes, unconvinced.

"So I mean it. Get out," Harper told them. "Or I'll be late."

"Whatever you say, Grace," Kane agreed, grabbing Kaia and backing out of the room. "Who am I to stand in the path of true lust?"

Harper sighed, and waited for the door to close so she could crawl back into bed, blissfully undisturbed. On second thought—

"Kane?" she called, just as he was about to disappear down the hall. He popped his head back in, and Harper forced herself to smile. "Leave the vodka."

"I can't wait to see the look on her face when she reads this," Miranda Stevens crowed, putting the finishing touches on their masterpiece. "She'll be out for blood."

"Too bad she already sucked us dry," Beth Manning pointed out. She laughed bitterly.

The flyer had been Miranda's idea. She'd been thirsty for revenge against Harper. Beth still had no idea why Miranda was so eager to take down her former best friend, and she didn't really care—Beth had more than enough reasons of her own to go after Haven High's reigning bitch.

And Harper was only the first name on a long list of enemies.

There was Adam Morgan, who was supposed to be the

love of her life. Too bad he'd turned out to be a lying hyp-
ocrite, accusing her of cheating when he was the one
who'd slept with another girl.

Then there was Kaia Sellers . . . the other girl.

Last—and least—there was Kane Geary, whose lies
she'd been dumb enough to believe and whose kisses she'd
been weak enough to accept.

Sweet, innocent Beth, who rescued spiders and cried at
the sappy reunions in long-distance commercials, now
hated them all, and none more than Harper Grace, the one
pulling the strings.

"All they care about is what people think of them,"
Miranda had pointed out, "so we flush their reputations
and that's it—they're finished."

"Any chance you want to tell me why you're doing
this?" Beth asked now.

"Now why would I do that," Miranda replied, pulling
her chair up to the computer, "when I could tell you about
the time in eighth grade when Harper laughed so hard at
the movies, she wet her pants?" Miranda shook her head,
almost fondly, and began to type. "I had to call her mother
on a pay phone to tell her to bring a new pair of under-
wear when she picked us up. And meanwhile . . ." Miranda's
voice trailed off as she concentrated on typing up the story.

"Meanwhile what?" Beth urged her, choking back
laughter.

"Meanwhile, Harper was inside the theater, crawling
around on the floor so that the usher wouldn't spot her and
throw her out. Eventually I had to fake an asthma attack—
you know, create a diversion so she could get out without
anyone spotting her."

"Lucky for her you were there," Beth marveled.

"Yeah?" The fond smile faded from Miranda's face. She turned away from Beth and stared at the screen, her fingers clattering loudly against the keyboard. "Yeah, I guess it was."

Cool.

Reed Sawyer hung up the phone and kicked his feet up on the rickety coffee table—really a row of old milk crates held together with superglue and chewing gum. He brought the joint to his lips and drew in a deep breath, closing his eyes as the searing sensation filled his lungs.

She couldn't stay away from him, that was clear.

Very cool.

"Dude, who was it?" his drummer asked, leaning his head back against the threadbare couch. "You look weird."

"Blissed out," the bass player agreed, taking the joint from Reed's outstretched fingertips. "Who's the chick?"

"No one," Reed mumbled.

"It was *her*," the drummer guessed, eyes gaping, and now he leaned forward on the couch. "Wasn't it? The rich bitch?"

"Don't call her that," Reed snapped, the words slipping out before he could stop them.

Damn.

Now they would all know.

"What are you doing with her, dude?" the bass player asked, shaking his head. "Girl like that? She's out of your league."

Let's see: silky jet-black hair, long lashes, designer clothes perfectly tailored to her willowy physique, the smoothest skin he'd ever touched . . . yeah, as if he needed a reminder that she was out of his league.

"What the hell do you know?" Reed asked, his voice lazy and resigned. It wasn't just the foggy halo clouding his mind or the buzz still tingling in his fingers that kept his anger at bay. It was the fact that the guys were right. As if it wasn't obvious that a grungy high school dropout-to-be and the pretty East Coast princess didn't belong together. Not to mention the fact that she *was* a bitch. She treated him like he was scum and obviously thought his friends were a waste of oxygen. But still—

They fit.

"Whatever," he said, standing up. Slowly. "I'm out of here."

"We've got rehearsal," the bass player reminded him.

"Do it without me," Reed said shortly, knowing it didn't matter. Every week, they got together to "rehearse." And every week, their instruments remained piled in the corner, untouched.

Reed had resolved that tonight, they would actually play a set. But that was hours ago, before things got fuzzy— and before she had called. He threaded his way through the ramshackle living room the guys had set up, filled with furniture snagged from the town dump and empty pizza boxes no one could be bothered to throw out.

"Just forget her, dude!" one of the guys called after him. "She'll mess you up!"

Reed just shrugged. Everything in his life was a mess; this thing with Kaia, whatever it was, would fit right in.

"I never . . ." Kaia paused, trying to come up with something suitably exotic. That was the problem with this game.

Once you'd done everything, there was nothing left to say. "I never got arrested."

She wasn't surprised when Reed took a drink. That was the rule: If you'd done it, drink up. And of course he'd been arrested. He was that kind of guy.

"For what?" she asked, leaning toward him.

They were perched on the back of his father's tow truck, at the fringe of a deserted mining complex. It was the place they'd come on their first date . . . if you could call it that.

Reed just pressed his lips together and shook his head.

"You're not going to tell me?"

He shook his head again. Big surprise. He didn't talk much. In fact, he didn't seem to do much of anything besides smoke up, hang out with his grease monkey friends, and stare at Kaia with an intense gaze that stole her breath.

He was beneath her—just like the rest of this town, this hellhole she'd been exiled to for the year. He was nothing. Dull. Deadbeat. Disposable. Or at least he should have been.

They rarely talked. Sometimes they kissed. Often, they just sat together in the dark, breathing each other in.

It was crazy.

And it was fast becoming her only compelling reason to make it through the day.

"I never," he began, putting down his shot glass. "I never kissed you here."

"Liar." Kaia caught her breath as he put his arms around her waist and kissed the long curve of her neck.

"How about here?" he murmured, lightly grazing his

tongue along her skin and nibbling her earlobe.

She closed her eyes and sighed heavily.

As if from a great distance, she could hear her cell phone ringing and knew who it would be. Was it only a few weeks ago that Jack Powell had seemed the consummate prize? The handsome, mysterious French teacher who was totally off limits and totally unable to resist her—he had it all, just as Reed had nothing. So why let the phone ring and ring? Why let Powell sit in his squalid bachelor pad, wondering and waiting, while she hooked up on the back of a pickup truck?

Kaia didn't know.

But with Reed's arms wrapped tightly around her, his curly black hair brushing her cheek, she also didn't care.

*Dear Adam, I know you said you never wanted to hear from me again.*

Adam Morgan held the match over the letter and paused for a moment, mesmerized by the dancing orange flame. It burned so brightly in the desert night. He dropped the flame into the darkness—and watched it spread.

*I'm sorry. I know I've said it before, and you won't listen—but I'm not going to stop. I can't, not until . . .*

The envelope had arrived on his doorstep after dinner. She hadn't even had the courage to stick around. Probably too afraid of what he'd say. But Adam had promised himself that he wouldn't say anything at all. Not ever.

*I know you think I betrayed you—betrayed what we had. But you have to understand, it's only because I love you. And you love me, I know you do.*

He hadn't bothered to read it. He wouldn't give her the

satisfaction. Instead, he'd climbed into his car and driven out of town, down a long stretch of deserted highway. He'd pulled over to the side of the road and climbed out. Scrambled over pebbles and spiny cactus brush, with nothing to light his way but the crescent moon. Fifty yards into the wilderness, he'd stopped. Crushed the letter and flung it to the ground.

Lit the match.

*If you would just let me explain, Adam. I* had *to get you away from her. She wasn't right for you. She couldn't give you what I could. She couldn't love you like I did. Like I do. We've been friends forever—more than friends. You can't give up on us. I can't. I* won't.

The flame was slow, almost deliberate. It ate into the letter, blackening the edges. The pages curled in the heat. The letters swam in front of his eyes, nothing more than meaningless black crawls. None of her words meant anything now; everything she'd told him over all these years had added up to nothing but lies.

For a moment, Adam was tempted to stick his hand in the flame. Maybe a physical pain, torn and blistering flesh, would steal his attention from the other, deeper pain that refused to go away. But he kept his hand still. And the letter burned.

*I'll keep apologizing until you hear me. Until I can make you understand. I can be a better person. I can be anyone you need me to be. But I can't do it without you.*

The letter was almost fully consumed. Adam was getting cold, and knew he could stop now, stomp out the fire, and leave the remaining fragments for the animals and the elements.

But he waited, and the fire burned on.

*I miss you—don't you miss me?*

And on.

*I need you. We need each other.*

And on.

*Please.*

And then there was just one smoldering fragment left, curling into the flame.

*Love forever,*

*Harper*

Adam stamped out the glowing pile of ashes and walked away.

# chapter

## 2

Beth held herself perfectly still, hoping he would change his mind and disappear. She didn't want to have to speak, but doubted she'd be able to force herself to stay silent. She didn't want to cry, or give him any indication whatsoever that she still cared, because, of course, she did. And more than anything, she wanted to stop.

"Hi," Adam said softly, sliding into the empty seat to her left.

If only the assembly would begin. Then there would be no chance for conversation, and Beth could pretend he wasn't there.

She hadn't looked in his direction yet, but she'd felt him hovering, wondering whether or not to sit down. Despite everything he'd done, it was as if a part of them was still connected. And maybe that was why she couldn't resist sneaking a glance at him out of the corner of her eye, longing to smooth down the windblown tufts of blond hair.

With a few words, she could have him back. "I forgive you." That's all it would take, and she could curl up against him again, his arms warm and strong around her. She could be a "we" again.

But she'd promised herself she would never forgive him—and unlike Adam, she kept her promises.

"You're not going to talk to me?" he asked.

Let him figure that one out for himself.

"At least *look* at me!"

Her lip trembled. *I will* not *cry,* she told herself.

"Fine," he spit out. She could tell he was struggling against his temper. "Then just listen." It's not like she had much of a choice—but it was a long time before he spoke again.

"I don't know what I'm supposed to say," he whispered as he reached for her hand. She whipped it away, afraid that if she let him touch her, or if she looked into his clear blue eyes, her anger might drain away.

She willed the principal to take the stage and begin the assembly; it was her only escape.

"What do you want from me?" Adam pleaded. "I said I'm sorry. I told you it wasn't my fault—"

"And whose fault was it?" she snapped. This was good. The more he denied, the more he evaded his responsibility, avoided how much he'd hurt her, the angrier she got. And that made things so much easier.

"Kane's," he pleaded. "Kaia's . . . Harper's."

Beth flinched at the name. It was true, Harper had manipulated him—Adam had just been stupid enough to let her. It was Harper who'd convinced Adam that Beth was cheating on him. Harper who'd enlisted Kane to prey on Beth's weakness and dupe her into a relationship based on lies. And, of course, it was Harper who'd swooped in to collect her prize—Adam—after he'd dumped Beth.

But even Harper couldn't be blamed for the most painful betrayal of all. No one had forced Adam to sleep with Kaia. He had no excuse—he and Beth had been together, they'd been *happy*, and he'd knowingly destroyed it in one stupid night.

"Is that supposed to fix everything?" she finally asked. She still couldn't bring herself to look at him.

"I don't know. I just . . . I wanted you to know that I'm . . . I mean, if we could just—" He suddenly stopped, and then she did turn to face him. He was doubled over in his seat, his head plunged into his hands.

"Just stop," she begged, forcing herself not to lay her hand against his broad back.

"I can't."

"Why?"

"Because I still love you."

He said it in a pained, strangled voice, without lifting his head. Beth didn't know whether to laugh or cry. Once, those words had been able to fix anything. Now they just left her feeling emptier than before.

"I love you," he said again.

And now Beth did something she'd once vowed never to do, not to Adam.

"I don't care."

She lied.


In the old days, Miranda and Harper would have skipped the assembly, taking it as a good excuse to sneak off to the parking lot for a smoke-and-bitch session about their least favorite people (Meaning: 90 percent of the student body).

But these weren't the old days. Too bad Harper didn't seem to notice.

"Rand, let's get out of here, what do you say?"

Harper had popped up from behind her seat, and Miranda stifled the impulse to swat her away like a mosquito she'd just caught draining her blood.

"I'd say forget it," she replied wearily, wishing she had the discipline to keep her mouth shut. The silent treatment had never been her thing. It was hard enough to just stand her ground with Harper—she'd been forgiving her for years, like a bad habit. But this time . . .

All she had to do was picture Kane—his tall, lean body, his knowing grin, his silky voice—and after all those years of fantasizing, his image sprang easily to mind. As did the echo of Harper's promise: "You and Kane—it's a done deal. I swear."

And what had she done instead? Pushed him on Beth, all to serve her own agenda. It was all about Harper, and always had been.

Harper couldn't even be bothered to deliver a real apology. Sure, she'd groveled for a couple days, but when Miranda stood firm, she'd resorted to a bravado that was as insulting as it was ineffective. Miranda could barely stand to watch her, putting on this gruesome show as if nothing had ever happened.

"Go find someone else to screw over," Miranda snapped. "I'm done."

"That's great," Harper said. "Very nice way to treat your best friend. What ever happened to 'forgive and forget'?"

"Not my style," Miranda muttered.

"Right—as if you have any style."

Inside, Miranda cringed, and glanced down at her outfit, a plain white T-shirt and cheap Wal-Mart jeans. Same as yesterday, same as the day before. Five years as sidekick to Haven's alpha girl and Miranda had somehow remained, to the end, cool by association, and association only. But Harper had never before flung the bitter truth in her face.

"I'd rather have no style than no class," Miranda replied pointedly. Harper wanted to jab at a soft spot? Two could play that game. And Harper, who still longed for the days when her family had ruled the town, and still chafed at the humiliating turn the Graces had taken, from princely robber barons to penny-pinching dry cleaners—Harper was nothing if not class conscious.

"I have more class—"

"All *you've* got," Miranda interrupted, "is a reputation. For now."

"Is that a threat?" Harper sneered, and for the first time, Miranda knew how it felt to be on the other end of Harper's poisonous gaze. But it only strengthened her resolve. She'd been wondering whether the little revenge plot hatched with Beth was too much, had gone too far—what a waste of worry. Obviously, Harper had put their friendship behind her. Miranda could—and would—do the same.

"Give me a break," Harper continued, rolling her eyes. "As if anyone in this school would listen to anything you have to say."

Oh, they would listen.

And then Harper would pay.

"I'm proud and pleased today to make a supremely important announcement that will affect all of you in the student body of our fair Haven High."

Kaia wasn't paying much attention to the principal and her pompous speech. Principals were always going on about "supremely important"—aka supremely irrelevant—announcements. It was part of the job description, and Kaia was content to hold up the students' end of the bargain: ignoring every word that came out of the principal's mouth.

But today she was putting on a good show of listening raptly—it was the best way to avoid Jack Powell's wandering eye.

"I have just learned that Haven High will be receiving a great honor. The governor of the esteemed state of California is setting off on a tour of the region's finest educational institutions, and he has decided to visit Haven High! Yes, the governor himself is arriving in two weeks for a *personal* inspection of our facilities."

Kaia would have snorted, were it ladylike to do so. The only state inspection this place deserved was the one that would condemn it. Peeling paint, creaky stairs, the mysterious stench that refused to dissipate—Haven High was a toxic waste dump masquerading as a high school.

With a few shining exceptions . . .

He was startlingly handsome, she'd give him that, she thought, watching Powell mingle with his balding, paunchy, middle-aged coworkers. He didn't belong here, not with his rakish smile, thick, wavy, chestnut hair, that arrogant smile and Jude Law accent. It had been such a turn-on, watching the other girls pathetically slobbering over him, and knowing that *she* was the one he'd chosen. Although technically, *she'd* chosen *him*—and, with a little prodding, he'd finally embraced his good fortune.

"In honor of the governor's arrival, one senior will be chosen by his or her peers to represent our fine school. He or she will deliver a speech on the subject of education— and I know he or she will do us all proud."

Kaia was proud of her catch, and would have loved to put it on display. But Jack Powell's policy was strict and unforgiving: In public, they ignored each other, without exception.

And yet, there he was, twenty rows ahead, craning his neck around and obviously searching for something—for Kaia. The irritated expression on his haughty face gave it away. She knew he hated the idea of chasing after anyone, but apparently he'd overcome his aversion: He'd left four messages on her voice mail since she'd ditched out on their last rendezvous, each one more incensed than the last.

"In preparation for the governor's arrival, I will be instituting a *no-tolerance* policy for all violations of school regulations. I expect you all will honor the rules as you always have, and *not* embarrass the administration or your-selves through any juvenile misbehavior."

Kaia, on the other hand, had always enjoyed the hunt. Extra points if she could break some rules in the process. Powell had been a special challenge, a cold, aloof trophy, whose acquisition had been fraught with the potential for scandal. Who'd have thought she be bored so quickly, will-ing to trade it all in for a greasy slacker in torn jeans, who reeked of pot and mediocrity?

"I look forward to reading your submitted speeches, and I know all of you at Haven High will look forward to this opportunity to shine for our state leadership. You'll do me, and yourselves, proud."

As the principal stepped down to a smattering of lackluster applause, Kaia grabbed her bag and slipped out the back of the auditorium. She knew Powell would never dare confront her on school grounds, much less in front of his boss—but why take a chance? She hadn't decided quite what to do with him yet, and didn't want to be forced into a decision. If the Reed thing blew over, it would be nice to have Powell ready and waiting on the back burner.

And if not . . . she'd let him down in her own time, and her own way. Gently.

Or, come to think of it, maybe not. After all, he liked it rough.

When the assembly ended, Beth zoned out for a moment, allowing herself to hope that her luck was about to change. If she was selected to deliver the speech to the governor, it could bulk up her college applications, and maybe even make up for her dismal SAT scores.

It was the first good news she'd gotten in weeks, and it gave her the strength to think about the future. She had to find a way to rebuild her life, without some guy to lean on. She'd done it before, but the prospect was still terrifying. Now, with this little kernel of confidence growing inside of her, maybe it was time to take the first step.

As the students filtered out of the auditorium, she followed a few feet behind a quiet, nondescript group of girls, careful not to let them notice her—but almost hoping they would. At least that would take the decision out of her hands.

She'd put this off for as long as she could, but being alone was just too hard. Miranda was useful, but she wasn't a friend. *Adam* had been a friend. As had the rest of his crowd, she'd thought, all the guys on the team, their girlfriends. Turns out, it was a package deal. Lose Adam, lose them all.

"Hey, guys. What's up?" She tried to make her voice sound nonchalant, smiling as if it had been only days since she'd last spoken to them and not—had it been weeks? Months?

"Beth?" Claire spoke first, as she always did. The other girls just stared at her with a mixture of hostility and confusion Beth recognized instantly. It was the look Beth had always flashed when one of the Haven elite had deigned to speak to her, inevitably with some kind of demand disguised as a not-so-polite request: *Let me borrow your history notes. Let me copy your physics homework. Let me have the key to the newspaper office so I can hook up with my boyfriend.* Those people only talked to you when they needed you, she and her friends had agreed. *Those* people. She'd never imagined that she would be one of them.

"What do you want?" Claire added, already half turned away.

"I just thought—" Beth hesitated. What did she want? To go back in time? Back before she'd skipped Claire's Halloween party, to hang with her boyfriend, before she'd partnered up with Adam on the American history project, leaving Abbie to fend for herself? Before she'd abandoned their lunch table, skipped the annual anti–Valentine's Day moviefest, forgotten Claire's birthday even though they'd celebrated it together since sixth grade? "I thought maybe we could . . ." But she couldn't make herself finish the thought.

"Is it true you broke up with Adam because he slept with someone else?" Abbie suddenly asked. Beth took a sharp breath, and her eyes met Claire's briefly—she looked equally shocked. Then Claire looked away.

"That's so rude," Claire snapped at Abbie, who, Beth remembered, always did what Claire told her to. "You can't just ask incredibly personal questions like that to someone you *barely know.*"

Beth had known Abbie since they were parked in neighboring strollers at the Sun 'n' Fun Day Care Center fifteen years ago, and Claire knew it.

"That's okay," Beth mumbled. "I don't mind talking about it." A lie.

"I heard you dumped him for Kane," another girl piped up. She had mousy brown hair and a hideous orange sweater. *My replacement?* Beth wondered.

"No, she dumped him, too," Abbie corrected her, then looked over at Beth. "Uh, right?"

"I can tell you guys about it at lunch today," Beth offered tentatively. "If you want."

"We don't want to bother you—" Claire began.

"Awesome," Abbie and the mousy girl chorused over her. "We'll see you then."

Beth sighed, hoping Claire's frosty attitude would thaw by the time they hit the cafeteria. Otherwise, it was going to be a long and painful hour, rehashing her failed love life while squirming under Claire's hostile glare.

It wouldn't do much for Beth's appetite.

But then, neither would eating alone.

"Don't do that, Kane, it tickles!"

Ignoring her pleas, Kane picked up the wriggling brunette and hoisted her over his shoulder as she kicked her legs with mock distress.

"Put her down, Kane!" her little friend, a dainty redhead, shrieked. Kane knew it was only because she was eager for her turn.

"Calm down, ladies," he urged them, depositing the brunette back on the ground. He slung an arm around each of them, admiring the way his muscles bulged beneath his tight sleeves. The new weights were working already. "You know you love it."

"Whatever." The brunette giggled, shoving him. Once their bodies made contact, she didn't pull away.

"Say what you want," he allowed, "but I know you're thrilled to have me back on the market."

The redhead—or, more accurately, the *air*head—stood on her toes to give him a kiss on the cheek. "I just don't know why you stayed away for so long," she whispered, her breath hot against his neck.

Good question.

"So what happened?" the brunette asked, tickling the back of his neck. He jerked away. "We thought you were reformed."

"Player no more," her friend chimed in. "Beauty tamed the beast. What gives?"

So what now, the truth?

Right.

Like he'd ever admit that he'd been the one rejected by a nonentity like Beth, or that losing her had cost him something more than his reputation. He knew that with a few easy words he could turn this around and make it into a win, trashing Beth's rep and redeeming his own.

But he couldn't do it.

He had no regrets, he insisted to himself. He'd just done what was needed to get what he wanted, same as always. Beth was a big girl who could make her own choices—and, if only briefly, she'd chosen him.

"You can't fool me," she'd said once, kissing him on the cheek. "I know who you really are."

He'd almost been sorry to prove her wrong.

"Come on, Kane," the redhead pushed. "Dish us some dirt!"

But Kane just smiled mysteriously and tugged her toward him, wishing her hair was blond, her eyes blue and knowing. "What's the difference what happened?" he asked. "I'm here now—and so are you, which means every-one wins. Right?"

The girls exchanged a glance, then shrugged.

"We're happy if you're happy," the brunette concluded, rising on her tiptoes to kiss him on the cheek.

Kane forced a grin. He certainly *looked* happy—and isn't that what counts?

Harper didn't have the nerve to face Adam. But she couldn't stay away. She was too used to seeing him every day, telling him everything, depending on him. Now that he wasn't speaking to her, the days were incomplete. Harper felt as if she'd lost a piece of herself that only came alive in his presence.

And she had no one to blame but herself.

She'd positioned herself in a small alcove across from his locker, knowing he'd stop by on his way to basketball practice. She just wanted to see him. And if she watched from afar, she wouldn't have to face that accusing look in his eyes.

She just hadn't counted on him spotting her.

"So what, you're following me now?" he growled, turning his back on her and throwing his stuff into the locker.

And there it was, that look in his eyes, as if she were a stranger, someone he wished he'd never met. Harper had tried to bluff her way through her encounter with Miranda, pretend that she didn't care about what happened between them—but when it came to Adam, she didn't have the strength for that kind of lie.

"Ad, I know you don't want to talk to me—"

"So why the hell are you here?" He slammed the locker shut, but kept his back to her. She took a small step in his direction, then another.

*Because I can't stay away.*

*Because I need you.*

*Because you need me.*

"Because I have to tell you I'm sorry."

"Trust me," Adam said gruffly. "You've said enough."

No. She'd begged him to stay. She'd left him unanswered voice mails, written letter after letter, but she'd never stood across from him and apologized for what she'd done. She'd never had the nerve. Harper Grace, who could say anything to anyone, had been too afraid to speak.

Was she sorry for what she'd done?

The elaborate plan had given her Adam, opening his eyes to the possibility of the two of them being more than friends. It had pried him away from his bland, blond girlfriend and made him realize that puppy love was no substitute for the real thing.

And when it all came crashing down, it had guaranteed that he would never trust her again.

"I *am* sorry," she said, hoping to convince herself as much as him.

He kept his back to her, placing both hands flat against the wall of lockers. His shoulders rose and fell as he took several deep, slow breaths. Harper couldn't tear her eyes from the fuzzy blond hair at the nape of his neck—she used to love to run her finger across it, making him shiver.

"I'm sorry," she said again. She came closer, but even as she stood just behind him, close enough to touch, he didn't turn. He must have known she was there, but he didn't move away. "Adam." She put her hand on his back, ran it lightly up toward his bare neck. It felt so good to touch him again. "Please . . ."

"Harper, *don't,*" he said, a low current of anger running through his voice. His fingertips turned white as he pressed them against the wall. "Just walk away." He slammed his right palm flat against the locker, and a sharp crack echoed through the empty hall. "Go. Please."

Adam would never hurt her—but, suddenly, Harper was afraid. She put her hand down and watched his frozen form for a moment.

Then she walked away.

Harper didn't lose. She got what she wanted, without exception. She didn't give up, ever.

But maybe this time, she had no choice.

"And what are *you* wearing?" Kaia asked, trying to keep the phone from slipping through her wet fingers as she sank lower into the hot tub. "Oooh, sexy."

She'd cancelled yet another rendezvous with Powell, but the man was insatiable—and so she'd given in to a little foreplay by phone. Thirty seconds in and she was already bored out of her mind; even that sexy British accent, describing where he would touch her and how, had lost its ability to thrill.

Kaia stretched a long, bare leg up into the air, enjoying the bite of the cool wind against her skin. She closed her eyes, straining to pay attention, wishing she could just tune out Powell's prattling and enjoy the silence of twilight.

Though she would never admit it to her father—and he would never bother to ask—there was one thing she appreciated about this desert hellhole: sunsets. Spectacular splashes of pink and orange, a blazing ball of reddish yellow sinking beneath the haze, lighting up the open sky. Best of all were the moments just after the sun disappeared beneath the horizon, and the sky gradually darkened, pinks fading to purples and blues until the first stars broke through the dark fabric of the sky.

"What? Oh yes, it feels good. Great," she said quickly, trying to sound enthused (though not trying too hard). "And if you just moved your hands down, and then I—" She sighed. "You know what? I'm just not feeling it."

Powell grumbled, but Kaia was done with him for the

night. And finally, after she'd agreed to model her new Malizia bikini for him in person sometime soon, he let her go.

She hung up the phone, but before laying it down on the deck, had a better idea. She dialed Reed's number and held her breath, surprised by how much she suddenly wanted him to answer.

But the phone rang and rang, and eventually Kaia gave up. She slid down farther and farther into the water, until only the tip of her nose and her dark eyes hovered above it. Kaia never let herself depend on anyone, and so she wouldn't let it bother her that Reed was unavailable. Still she couldn't help wondering where he was . . . and whether he was thinking of her.

Adam blew off practice.

He had to.

Once, basketball had been an escape, a way to get out of his own head and relax into the rhythm of running, leaping, throwing, pushing himself to the limit. It had been a refuge.

And then Kane joined the team.

These days, Adam didn't have the energy to sink many shots or work on his passing. Every ounce of strength was devoted to resisting the temptation to bash in Kane's smug face, and pay him back for ruining Adam's life.

Only, after the encounter with Harper, Adam didn't have much strength left.

So he ditched practice, seeking a new refuge from the mess he'd made of his life. He needed to turn off his brain, and the 8 Ball, a dank pool hall at the edge of town, was the perfect place to do it.

It was dark, even during the day—black boards over the windows ensured that no afternoon light would slip in and disturb the handful of surly regulars. It was a place to hide. And, with five-dollar pitchers, a place to forget.

He'd come here with Harper once, and she'd put on a disgusting show, throwing herself at the sleazy goth bartender. Maybe it should have been a sign. But Adam had ignored the warning, and instead dumped a pitcher of beer on the bartender's head in a jealous rage. The bartender had vowed to make him sorry if he ever returned—and so, since then, Adam had known to stay away.

But Adam was tired of doing what was good for him— things managed to blow up in his face, anyway. So why bother?

"Can I get a Sam Adams?" he asked the bartender. It was the same guy. Good.

"Don't I know you?" the loser asked, pushing his greasy hair out of his eyes to get a better look.

"Is that supposed to be a pickup line?" Adam asked sarcastically. "Because trust me, I'm not interested."

"You're the asshole," the bartender exclaimed. As if, in a place like this, that was a distinguishing characteristic.

"Who are you calling an asshole?" Adam stood up and gripped the edge of the bar. All the emotion that had been simmering within him finally rose to the surface—and in a moment, he knew, he could give it permission to explode.

"I thought I told you never to come back here," the scrawny weasel complained. He turned away. "I'm not serving you. Get out."

"Or what?" Adam growled.

"Or I'll call the cops on your underage ass. In fact, maybe I'll do it, anyway, just for fun."

Adam flexed his muscles.

Made a fist.

Pulled back, and—

Stopped.

If he let himself lose control, he might never get it back again.

So instead of smashing in the bartender's face, he grabbed a glass from the bar and threw it, hard as he could, to the ground.

"What the hell are you doing?" the bartender cried, as glass sprayed across the floor.

"I have no fucking idea," Adam said honestly, and walked out. There were plenty of other bars in town, plenty of cheap drinks. Plenty of ways to forget.

And that was exactly what he needed.

If it was too dangerous to let himself react, then—at least for one night—he could let himself drown.

She was like a statue in the moonlight, pale, graceful, glowing in the night. He sucked in a sharp breath, forcing his body to stay calm. He couldn't afford to give himself away.

She was so close—and it was so hard not to reveal himself, and take possession of her. As was his right.

He'd been with her before; he would be again. But nothing was more delicious than watching from a distance, knowing that she belonged to him.

She climbed out of the hot tub, and he held his breath. This was the moment he'd been waiting for. Her perfect, glistening body, slicing through the air, every step precise, premeditated. As she toweled herself off, shivering, she suddenly froze, staring out into the darkness.

He froze, too, and it felt as if their eyes had locked. Had she sensed his invisible presence? His heart slammed in his chest, and his fingers tightened against the fence post he'd crouched behind. Moments like this—the threat of being caught, the chill of a near miss—made the game worth playing.

But he'd learned well how to minimize the risks, and knew she would never catch on. Nothing was sweeter than facing her day in and day out, knowing that she could never imagine what lay behind his mask.

She liked to think she didn't trust anyone, but she trusted him. She underestimated him, and he allowed it.

For now.

# chapter

# 3

They'd decided to go old school.

E-mail would have been more efficient, and a Web site might have been snazzier, but after serious consideration, Beth and Miranda had decided that neither had the technical prowess to put something like that together undetected. And plausible deniability was key.

E-mails could be traced. Circuits always led back to their source. But paper was untraceable—and as editor in chief of the school paper, Beth had access to all the printing equipment she needed.

She pulled the stack of flyers out of the printer as Miranda ejected their disk and wiped their work from the computer's memory.

"Behold," said Beth, holding up the crimson sheet crammed with dirty little secrets. "Our masterpiece."

Miranda grabbed a copy and quickly scanned the elegantly designed layout.

"Unbelievable, isn't it, that they were able to accomplish so much in their short, sordid lives?"

"I'm not sure *'accomplish'* is the right word," Beth said, reading out a few of her favorites. "*'HG used to steal money from the collection plate. AM is impotent. KG is afraid of the dark.'* I'm not sure what it is they've accomplished."

"Other than making asses of themselves," Miranda said, and laughed. "Well, thanks to us."

They'd included some gossip about a bunch of randoms, too, just for cover. But that was a diversion. Soon everyone would know that KG was so desperate, he had to trick girls into sleeping with him; that sometimes HG still stuffed her bra. Neither Miranda nor Beth knew much about the mysterious new girl from the East Coast, but before everything came down, Harper had passed along a bit of juicy info about Kaia and Haven High's resident pothead that was too weird not to be true.

"Are we really doing this?" Beth asked, as she split the pile in half and handed one stack to Miranda. It was almost 6 A.M., which meant there'd be plenty of time to spread them all over school before even the most diligent early bird appeared for his worm.

"Definitely." Miranda swung her long, reddish hair over her shoulder and looked defiantly up at Beth. "It's exactly what they deserve."

"I guess . . ."

"No second thoughts," Miranda ordered. "They screwed us. Both of us. Because they thought we'd put up with it."

And Beth remembered the surprise in Kane's eyes when she'd pushed him away for the last time. The mocking look in Harper's every time Beth dared confront her, as if knowing that sweet, quiet Beth would always be the one to back down first. And she remembered the way Adam had treated her when he'd thought she was the cheater, his cold, unrelenting cruelty, the unwillingness to bend, to trust, to forgive.

Now *she* was supposed to just get over it? Because betraying Beth, well, that didn't really count?

"You take the science wing, I'll hit the lockers by the cafeteria," Beth said determinedly. Forget moving on. Forget backing down.

"That's better," Miranda cheered, locking up behind them. "Let's get this done."

*Did you hear?*

*Is it true?*

*I heard he was a virgin when he slept with Kaia.*

*And when she blew him off, he cried.*

*Well, I heard Kane wanted Beth so much he posed naked with Harper and they doctored the photos.*

*They didn't just pose—he and Harper totally did it on the locker room floor.*

*No, I heard it was on the soccer field, and Kaia was in it too. Threesome, baby.*

*So who was taking the pictures?*

*Could Kaia really be hooking up with that skeezy stoner?*

*Didn't you hear? She's a total nympho.*

*Why do you think they threw her out of her last school?*

*Did he really—?*

*And then she—?*

*How could they—?*

*I don't believe it, but . . .*
*You won't believe it, but . . .*
*It doesn't make any sense, but . . .*
*Trust me.*
*It's true.*

"Oooh, Harper, you must be soooo humiliated!"

Harper rolled her eyes. She'd been (barely) tolerating her lame sophomore wannabe-clone for months now, but the Mini-Me act was getting old. Especially now that the girl had dug up the nerve to speak to her in public. As if Harper was going to dent her own reputation by acknowledging Mini-Me's existence—or, worse, giving people the impression that they were actually *friends.*

"We just want you to know we're *there* for you," Mini-Me's best friend gushed. Harper couldn't be bothered to remember her name, either, and since the girl was decked out in the same faux BCBG skirt and sweater set that Harper had ditched last season, Mini-She would suffice.

"What are you talking about?" she hissed, through gritted teeth. Under normal circumstances she would have just closed her locker and walked away. But something strange was going on today. She'd been getting weird looks all morning, and once, difficult as it was to believe, it had almost seemed like someone was laughing—at *her.*

"Oh, Harper, we don't believe any of it," Mini-Me assured her.

"Of course not," Mini-She simpered, her head bouncing up and down like a bobblehead doll. "Well, except that thing about—"

"None of it," Mini-Me said firmly, giving Mini-She an obvious *shut your mouth* glare.

"None of what?" Harper was getting increasingly irritated by the twin twits—and by the sensation that something very bad was about to happen. Or had already happened, without her knowing it, which was worse. Harper owned this school, and *nothing* happened without her say-so.

"You mean you haven't . . ." Mini-Me's eyes lit up. She tried to force a concerned look, but her eagerness was painfully clear. "Oh, I *hate* to be the one to show you this, but . . ." She pulled a folded red flyer out of her back pocket. Harper had seen them floating around that morning, but assumed it was just another lame announcement about the next chess club tournament or some charity drive for the community service club. "Maybe I shouldn't show it to you," Mini-Me said, waving the folded flyer out of Harper's reach.

"But at least we can be there for her, when she sees it." Mini-She patted Harper's shoulder, and Harper squirmed away with a grimace. "We'll *always* be there for you, Harper, no matter what anyone else says."

"You've always got us," Mini-Me agreed. "I mean, we don't care if you wet your pants or slept with a million guys or—"

"Give me that," Harper snarled, snatching the flyer out of Mini-Me's hand. She unfolded it slowly, forcing her hands not to shake.

The words leaped off the page.

All her darkest secrets, all her most embarrassing moments, her deepest fears, all laid out in black print, stretching across the page for anyone to see. It had been published anonymously—the coward's way—but Harper didn't need a byline to know whom to blame. There was only one person who knew all her secrets—the one person she had trusted never to betray her.

Harper smiled, though it felt more like a grimace of horror. Hopefully the Minis would be too dim to tell the difference. Then she shrugged. "Is this all?"

"*All?*" Mini-Me squealed. "Don't you get it? 'HG'— Harper Grace. That's *you*."

Harper rolled her eyes, almost thankful for the Minis' presence; the familiar sense of disgust was helping her suppress all those less desirable emotions. Helplessness. Humiliation. Despair.

*Focus on something more constructive,* she warned herself. *People can only hurt you if you let them. Don't be a victim.*

"See?" Mini-She chirped. "Like it says right here, 'HG was so desperate for AM that she . . .'"

Harper tuned her out—after all, she already knew the story. It was more important to regain her focus and start working on damage control. But cool, calculating strategy was impossible when one unquestionable fact kept drilling into her brain.

Miranda had betrayed her. No one else knew what she knew.

She wouldn't have done it on her own, Harper was certain of that. She didn't have this kind of nastiness in her. She would have been goaded into it by someone else, someone so pure and innocent that no one would ever suspect her of spewing such poison.

"What are we going to do?" Mini-Me moaned. As if there were a "we."

"Who needs to do something?" Harper asked, crumpling the flyer into a ball and tossing it over her shoulder like the trash it was. "You know what they say, there's no such thing as bad publicity."

"You don't even care?" Mini-She asked, eyes wide and adoring. From the expression on the Minis' faces—impressed and totally devoid of pity—Harper grew certain that she'd be able to fix this.

These last few weeks had been the most lonely and miserable of Harper's life—something like this could have been a fatal blow. And yet, she marveled, perhaps Beth had done her a favor. Because she suddenly felt invigorated. She felt offended and insulted, righteous and wronged, empowered and enraged.

She felt like herself again.

And it felt good.

Beth and Miranda met up in the second-floor girls' bathroom after third period to compare notes. The school was buzzing about the already legendary flyer—half the student body had memorized it, and the other half had used it as a springboard to create and pass along wildly unlikely rumors of their own.

"I can't believe we actually did it," Miranda whispered, checking under the stalls to make sure they were really alone.

"You should have—" Beth quickly stopped talking as two babbling juniors burst through the door. Miranda turned on the faucet, pretending to wash her hands, while Beth peered into the streaked mirror, applying a new coat of transparent lip gloss.

"You think she, like, did it to herself?" the tall brunette asked, smoothing down her hair and using her pinkie to rub in some garish blue eye shadow. "But, like, why?" She dug through her overstuffed silver purse and pulled out a large gold hoop, wide enough to fit around her wrist, and clamped it onto her earlobe.

"Oh, puh-leeze," the shorter, pudgier one said, locking herself inside an empty stall. Her bright yellow platform shoes tapped against the linoleum. "She's mad crazy for attention, you know she'd do anything."

"But we're talking total humiliation hot zone—"

"Massive meltdown territory, but does she seem upset? Negative. You know she's, like, loving every minute of it."

"I don't know," the tall one said, now perched on the sink, fiddling with her nails, which were painted cotton candy pink and so long that they almost curled back toward her fingertips. "Maybe it was some nobody, like, you know, some bitter loser who wanted—"

"As if." A laugh floated out of the stall. "How would some loser know all of that? No, it had to be—"

Finally, Miranda couldn't help herself. "Did you ever think that maybe—"

"Uh, excuse me?" the brunette said, glaring. "Were we talking to you?"

The shorter girl burst out of the stall and quickly slathered on a layer of hot pink lipstick. She didn't bother to look in Miranda's direction—or make a move toward the sink. "Was she, like, eavesdropping on our conversation?"

"Whatever. Forget her."

"Her who?" the other girl cackled as she pushed

through the girls' room door, the brunette following close behind.

Miranda and Beth stared at each other for a moment, then burst into laughter. "Were they for real?" Beth asked in wonderment.

"Oh, yeah, like, totally, I mean, you know, whatever," Miranda said, giggling. "For reals, dude."

"And that makes *us* the losers?" Beth asked, grinning.

"Apparently." Miranda stuck out her hand to shake. "Nice to meet you, I'm nobody. And who are you?"

"Someone who would *never* walk out of this bathroom without washing her hands," Beth joked.

"I think we're missing the key point here," Miranda said, trying to stop laughing. "Did you hear the way *they* were talking about *'her'*?"

"Harper," Beth filled in.

"Right. Obviously. Like she was this pathetic nonentity, desperate for attention. . . ."

"Humiliated," Beth said, raising her eyebrows.

"Pitiful," Miranda added, shaking her head.

"Defeated."

Miranda grinned and slung an arm around Beth's shoulders. "And all by a pair of bitter nobodies. Who would've thought?"

The curiosity-seekers had been swarming Kane all morning—and by lunchtime, it seemed half the school had surrounded him, desperate for insider information and some notoriety-by-association. Outwardly, he smiled, preening under the attention. But underneath, he was fuming. It was Beth. It had to be. No one else could know some of the things she'd printed, the few secrets he'd been foolish enough to share.

That was the worst of it: the realization that he'd brought this on himself. After swearing to protect himself, he'd left himself raw and exposed.

Not again—never again.

After spotting the flyer, Kane had quickly started his own campaign of disinformation; judging from Kaia's and Harper's animated smiles and the naked curiosity of their eager disciples, it seemed the girls had chosen to do the same. They sat at separate tables, each the center of a small whirlpool of people, flowing past to catch a moment with the stars. The horde surrounding Kane was, of course, the largest.

"She begged me to take her back," he confided to the second-string point guard. "It was getting pathetic. I mean, tears is one thing—you know girls. But when she started showing up at my house in the middle of the night? It's not like I *wanted* to call the cops. . . ."

"Let's just say, I now have a pretty good idea of what it must feel like to kiss a cold, dead fish," he confided to the sympathetic blonde from the cheerleading squad.

"And the smell . . . you know, she works at that diner, and all the onions, the grease, the sweat . . ." He shook his head, and the busty freshman patted him sweetly on the shoulder. "It was nauseating. I have a very delicate stomach, you know, and sometimes . . ."

"Sure, *she* couldn't get enough of it," he bragged to the gawky junior who managed the basketball team. "But what was I supposed to do? She was—well, let's just say Adam's pretty lucky he never made it to home base."

He almost felt sorry for Beth. She was like a dolphin, playing at being a shark. Which was a dangerous game: You were likely to get eaten.

The note the teacher had handed her had been short and sweet: *Report to my classroom. Now.*

Okay, maybe not so sweet.

"Jack," Kaia said simply, stepping into his empty classroom and closing the door behind her. "Bonjour."

Powell was perched on the edge of his desk, fingering a red sheet of paper. Kaia recognized it immediately, with little surprise.

"You said you'd stopped seeing him," Powell said coldly, placing the flyer carefully down on the desk. "I thought I'd made my position perfectly clear: I don't like to share."

Kaia strode toward him and took a seat at one of the desks in the front row, aware that his gaze was glued to her long, tan legs, barely covered by a green suede miniskirt.

"Do you really want to discuss this *here,* Jack?" It was a violation of every rule he'd set for them, and it stank of desperation.

"There's nothing to discuss. You told me you'd stopped. You told me you wouldn't, with—*that.* And now I read . . ."

Kaia laughed. "Are you going to believe some piece of trash you probably confiscated from one of your clueless freshmen? Just how gullible are you?"

Powell's skin turned slightly red, whether in anger or embarrassment, Kaia couldn't be sure. She could put him out of his misery right now, confess to the dalliance with Reed, and suggest he find himself another student to play with—or maybe even pick on someone his own age. But Kaia wasn't quite ready to finish things, and she *certainly* wasn't going to let some loser with a printer and a grudge force her hand.

She got up and walked slowly to the door, as if to leave, then paused with her hand on the knob. "Do I really need to defend myself?" Kaia asked. "Or can we stop this game and play another . . . ?"

Powell hopped off the desk, walked toward her, and then did something he'd never done before on school grounds. He touched her.

Placing his hand over hers on the doorknob, he turned the lock.

"We can table this for now," he told her, his lips inches from the nape of her neck, his fingers digging into her skin. "You're a smart girl, Kaia. You know better than to screw this up. Take this as a warning."

He pulled her roughly toward him, and she let him, hyperaware of the people in the hallway, just on the other side of the door. Only a few inches separated them from discovery, a thought that turned her on far more than Powell's hands roaming across her body.

Yes, Kaia was a smart girl, and she almost always knew better. She just never acted on it.

Where was the fun in that?

The whispers flew back and forth over Miranda's head. No one thought to ask her what was true—most likely, no one thought of her at all.

*Without Harper, I'm invisible,* she thought, pushing around the soggy food on her tray. She had no appetite.

Not when Harper was at the center of an admiring crowd, soaking in the attention. Miranda had just given her more of what she loved the most. From across the room, Miranda couldn't see the self-satisfied grin on Harper's face, but knew it was there. And she couldn't hear the spin Harper would put on everything to cast herself in a good light—but she knew Harper would. A spotlight. It all seemed so obvious now, that this was how their feeble plot was doomed to end.

Teaming up with Beth, blandest of the bland, to take on Haven High's dark queen? What had she been thinking?

Beth wasn't as bad as Miranda had always thought, and was probably undeserving of all the hours she and Harper had put into mocking her behind her back. (Miranda had long ago perfected her Beth imitation, which never failed to send Harper into uncontrollable gales of laughter.)

But "not that bad"? What good was that, when you were going up against someone who had It? Someone who could mold minds, bend wills, make the world into exactly what she wanted it to be. Harper had It, and Beth didn't. Neither did Miranda.

Together, they made one big, fat nothing, and Miranda was beginning to wonder if she might have been better off alone.

Spin control only took a small portion of Harper's attention, and she devoted the rest of it to watching Miranda, pathetically slumped over a table on the other side of the cafeteria. They'd fought before; their friendship was built on fights. But this was different.

Miranda could never hold a grudge—and so Harper had never had to worry that, eventually, all would be forgiven. She'd learned that lesson in sixth grade, when the two of them had their first huge fight while rehearsing their sixth-grade performance of *Macbeth* (suitably abridged for attention-deficit-disordered twelve-year-olds). It had started small: an argument over who got to use the "real" (plastic) sword and who would be stuck wielding a wrapping-paper tube covered with aluminum foil.

Harper won, of course, bringing up the unassailable point that the whole show was named after her character. It seemed only logical that she, as the star, get the best of everything—lines, costumes, makeup, and, of course, *swords*. But Miranda had given in grudgingly, and only after hours of endless argument; by the time Harper finally took the stage, plastic sword in hand, she and Miranda hadn't spoken for a week.

When the climactic scene arrived, Miranda had the first good line. "Turn, hellhound, turn!" she cried as Macduff, the one man destined to take down Macbeth.

Harper spun to face her challenger. They stared at each other across the stage, readying themselves for the sword fight, gritting their teeth and narrowing their eyes as if the fate of the kingdom truly lay on their shoulders. Their teacher had been very specific: Cross "swords" three times, and then Miranda would slice off Harper's head. In a manner of speaking, of course.

Miranda swung, Harper parried, jumped back, sliced her sword toward Miranda, who blocked the blow with her wrapping-paper tube and danced around the stage, taunting Harper under her breath.

And Harper, who'd been planning to lie down and deliver the greatest death scene Grace Elementary had ever seen, couldn't bring herself to lose the fight—and, by definition, her dignity—in front of all those people. She swung wildly, and Miranda's flimsy sword bent in two—at which point Miranda screeched in frustration and launched herself at Harper. The two of them stumbled to the ground, writhing and rolling across the stage, pinching and poking, tickling and tugging hair . . . until their eyes met and, simultaneously, they burst into uncontrollable giggles.

Harper and Miranda had spent that weekend in an intense, forty-eight-hour catch-up session, sharing every detail of the painful hours they'd spent not speaking to each other.

"I was sooooo bored," Miranda had complained.

"You were bored? I fell asleep standing up," Harper countered.

"I had to play Jeopardy Home Edition all night with my parents."

"I spelled out the names of everyone I know in alphabet soup."

"I missed you," Miranda had confessed, laughing.

Even then, Harper had known better than to confess that she'd missed Miranda more. They'd laughed about it for years, and sometimes even now when Harper was being particularly bitchy, Miranda would call her a "hellhound"; Harper always replied with her own favorite line: 'Lay on, Macduff, and damn'd be he that first cries, "Hold, enough!"' It was the code of their friendship, and its meaning was simple. They would never turn into their characters;

they would fight—but never to the death. They would always stop in time, just before landing the final blow.

But here she was, watching Miranda pick at her food, scared to go over to her, scared not to. If Harper stood over her pleading, "Lay on, Macduff"—meaning, *Yell at me, hit me, hate me, and then, please, forgive me*—would it fix anything?

Not likely, Harper decided—not if Miranda had been behind the gossip flyer. That was a death blow. Harper may not have seen it coming, but she knew when it was time to lay down her sword and leave the stage.

# chapter

## 4

"Okay girls, time for a vote: *13 Going On 30* or *The Princess Bride?*"

As *13 Going On 30* won by general acclamation, Beth tried to will herself to care. A few days ago, she would have said this was all she wanted—to be accepted back into the fold, to regress to the good ol' days of sleepover parties and road trips to the mall, popcorn and girl talk.

"Beth, can you grab us another bag of Hershey's Kisses?" Claire asked, and Beth traipsed upstairs, fighting against the suspicion that they'd start talking about her as soon as she was gone. They'd invited her, which was a step in the right direction—but no one seemed to particularly want her around.

"Have no fear, the chocolate's here," she said gamely, returning downstairs and pouring the Hershey's Kisses into a bowl.

"Great, let's stick in the movie," Claire suggested. Beth couldn't wait. As soon as the lights went out, she could drop the fake smile and stop trying to force perky conversation. She could let her mind wander and try to figure out exactly how she was going to make it through to graduation.

"Before we watch, I want to ask Beth something," one of the girls said eagerly. It was Leslie, the one Beth had come to think of as her replacement. Though had she ever been that timid and sallow? Claire rolled her eyes, but plopped down on the couch, defeated. "So . . . ," the girl continued. "What was it like?"

"What was *what* like?"

"*You* know," Abbie said. *"It."*

"You and Kane," Leslie pressed, "what was it like when you . . ."

"What was it like to have a boyfriend?" Beth asked incredulously. Yes, when she'd been part of this group, they'd all been single—but almost two years had passed. Since then, surely at least one of them had—

"Sex," Claire said harshly. "They want to know what it was like to have sex." She scowled at Beth, as if daring her to respond.

"But I—" Beth had been embarrassed by her virginal status for so long that she'd almost forgotten what it could be like, to be part of a group where there was no pressure to be someone you weren't or go somewhere you weren't ready to go. For the first time all night, she smiled a real smile. "I haven't," she explained, feeling a surge of relief that she could say the words without worrying that anyone would judge her. She'd forgotten what it was like to have girl friends—*real* friends. "I mean, Kane and I never—and neither did Adam and I, so I'm still a . . ."

"Virgin?" Claire snorted. "Yeah, right."

"I *am,*" Beth insisted, trying to ignore her.

"But, Beth," Abbie began hesitantly, "we've all heard . . . Kane said . . ."

"Kane's lying," Beth protested hotly. "Whatever he said, we never—"

"And *I* heard that you were the one who talked him into it," Leslie said. "That he wanted to take it slow, but— not that there's anything wrong with that," she added hastily, catching sight of Beth's expression.

"Leave her alone," Claire decreed, and Beth felt a brief stab of gratitude. Very brief, as Claire continued, "Obviously, she doesn't want to talk about it, not with *us*. No need to lie anymore, Beth. We'll just stop asking."

Beth kept the smile frozen on her face as Claire popped in the movie and the lights went out. It was only then, under the cover of laughter and music and inane dialogue, that Beth was able to move. She crept over their sprawled bodies, and up the stairs to the guest bathroom. Once inside, the door shut and locked behind her, she sat down on the toilet seat, put her head in her hands, and let the tears leak out.

She was losing control.

There were so many people she needed to be. With Adam, the bitter, unforgiving ex; with Harper, the tough rival; with her family, the reliable caretaker. She'd thought that with her old friends she could relax and just be herself, but they didn't want that. They wanted yet another Beth, a world weary refuge from the popular crowd who could give them the inside scoop on a world they'd never inhabit.

So many masks to wear, and none of them fit, not really. She didn't know who she was anymore—and she no longer had the energy to figure it out.

Harper was back. So much for skulking in the shadows and hiding under the covers. That wasn't going to get her anything. It wasn't going to get her Adam. And it wasn't going to get her revenge.

So Friday night, she'd whipped out her cell phone and called Kaia and Kane. It was time for a council of war, and these two were battle-tested.

"Nice to see you out of bed, Grace," Kane commented as they settled into a booth in the back of Bourquin's Coffee Shop.

"It's even nicer to see me in it," Harper quipped, "not that you'll ever know."

Kane grinned, and Kaia set down a tray of frothy iced coffees.

"And the plan is . . . ?" she began, arching an eyebrow.

"I thought that was your department," Harper joked—and then the smile faded from her face. After all, the last plan Kaia'd come up with had led to disaster. It had, ultimately, led them here.

"We all agree it was Beth?" Kane asked, delicately holding the notorious flyer between two fingers as if afraid to get his hands dirty.

"I still say she couldn't have done it alone," Kaia pointed out.

"She's very resourceful," Harper put in quickly. She'd deal with Miranda—her own way, in her own time.

"You're the one who always told me she was a waste of space," Kane reminded her.

"And *you're* the one who always told me I underestimated her," Harper argued. "Obviously you were right."

Kane closed his eyes and took a deep breath, as if inhaling her words. "Music to my ears. But you sound surprised—when are you going to learn that I'm always right?"

"So, Mr. Right," Kaia said, leaning forward eagerly. "You know her best—how do we take her down?"

Silence fell over the table.

"If we had proof, we could just turn her in," Harper mused. But there was no proof—and, besides, ratting her out to the authorities seemed such an inelegant solution. Why pass the buck to the administration when they could handle the problem themselves?

Kane put down his coffee and looked up at the girls, his lips pulling back into a cold smile. "I can tell you what her pretty little heart desires the most this week—"

"Not you," Kaia and Harper quipped at the same time. Their eyes met, and they burst into laughter. Kane's expression didn't change.

"If you two are done . . ."

The girls nodded, adopting identical *we'll be good* expressions.

"As I was *saying,* if I know Beth, there's only one thing she wants this week: something flashy that would impress colleges and cement her goody-goody rep once and for all . . ."

"She could prove to the whole school that she's the best," Kaia said thoughtfully.

"All the teachers would love her," Kane pointed out.

"And she'd get to feel like a VIP, superior to the rest of us," Kaia added, with a knowing smile.

"Well?" Harper asked in confusion, growing tired of the game. The two of them were having way too much fun stringing this out. *What?*"

"That speech for the governor," Kane explained. "I hear she's going for it, and she hasn't got any real competition. Unless . . ."

"Wouldn't it be a shame," Kaia picked up, "if someone stole it out from under her? Someone prettier, more popular, someone *she* probably thinks can't string two words together?"

"And maybe she finds out that she can't just flutter those blue eyes and get everything she wants," Kane concluded.

"Especially"—Kaia grabbed the flyer from him and tore it in two—"if she's going to play with fire."

"And exactly who do you—" Harper stopped as the obvious sunk in. "You want *me* to write the damn speech? Put on a show for the governor like the principal's trained monkey?"

"Who better to beat her out than her sworn enemy?" Kaia pointed out. "The one who already stole everything worth having?"

It did have a certain beauty to it.

And Harper did so love to win.

"Are you guys sure about this?" Harper asked.

"Second thoughts, Grace?" Kane asked, arching an eyebrow. "This was your idea."

"She tried to trash our lives," Kaia pointed out. "Yours, most of all."

Harper didn't want to say what she was thinking—that maybe Beth had lost enough.

"You know Adam would go back to her in a second," Kaia reminded her. "All she'd have to do is say the word. He thinks she's so pure, so innocent. . . ."

Beth had brought the fight to them, Harper reminded herself, and after all, what had she really lost? Kane was right: She could have Adam back whenever she wanted. *Harper* was the one left alone, groveling for forgiveness that might never come.

Didn't Beth expect a little payback for that? More to the point, didn't she deserve it?

"All right," Harper conceded. "I'm in. All in."

"Good decision," Kaia said, clinking her mug against Harper's. "To revenge."

"To winning," Kane added, clinking their glasses with his own.

Harper paused just before taking a sip, and added one more toast. "To justice."

Kaia checked her watch on the way out of the coffee shop. She had just enough time to head home and change, before meeting Reed. Or she could stop by Guido's Pizza early and see if he was ready for her. If not, she could at least sit there as he worked. She loved watching his sure movements behind the counter, tossing the dough, smearing the sauce across a fresh crust, sprinkling the cheese. She'd never thought fast-food preparation could be so hot.

She slid in behind the wheel of the BMW, but before she could decide which way to turn out of the lot, her cell phone rang.

"Good news. My dinner engagement has been cancelled. I'm free for the night. Be here in half an hour."

Kaia chewed on the corner of her lip and tapped her index finger against the phone. Powell liked to order her around. It gave him the illusion he was in control.

"Can't—plans," she said quickly.

"Forget them," he suggested. "I have a special treat for you."

For a moment, Kaia was tempted—but as she thought of Reed's lopsided grin, and the way his rumpled, curly hair always made it look like he'd just climbed out of bed, the temptation passed.

"Sorry," she told him, her flat tone making it clear that, as usual, she wasn't.

"What could be more important than a night with me?" Powell asked.

"What's the difference?" Kaia snapped, suddenly unwilling to make up a lie. This wasn't a relationship, after all—they were under no obligation to each other. That was the beauty of it, at least until he'd turned into the amazing human jellyfish, wrapping his tentacles around her at any opportunity for fear she'd slip away. "I'm not coming."

"*Tu me manques,*" Powell said. *I miss you.* "*Mon amour.*" *My love.* He knew very well that she couldn't resist when he spoke to her in French.

"I'll come now," she said with a sigh, regretting it almost as soon as the words were out of her mouth. "You've got twenty minutes."

"You say that now, but you know you won't want to leave." She could hear the smug grin behind his words and, as always, it repulsed her—and turned her on. "You know you can't say no to me."

"Twenty minutes. That's it."

Kaia clicked the phone shut, cutting off his laughter. So, new plan: two guys in one night. She'd double-dipped in the dating pool before, but this time felt different.

Kaia pulled out onto the road, turning toward Powell's dingy side of town. She refused to let herself slip into some kind of juvenile relationship, imagining that she and Reed were "going steady"—it was a slippery slope and, before you knew it, she'd likely be sucked into a downward spiral of gooey love poems, Valentine's Day candy, pathetic pop songs, and dithering about whether "he loves me" or "he loves me not."

*That* was unacceptable, and even if she didn't particularly *want* to see Powell tonight or suffer through his groping fingers and pompous Brit wit, she would, anyway, just as a reminder that she was free. Kaia had never let herself be obligated to anyone—as far as she was concerned, it was a step away from ownership, and no one owned her. No one ever would.

"Now *that* is a fine piece of ass!" The second-string point guard leaped out of his chair and pushed his way to the edge of the stage, waving a wad of dollar bills in the air.

Adam looked around the table searching for a bemused expression to match his own, but saw only naked desire in his teammates' eyes. So what was wrong with Adam? Three half-naked women dancing onstage a few feet away, their perfect bodies gyrating to a hard, driving beat—and all he could do was stare into his glass and wallow in his own pain?

"You're pathetic, man!" one of the guys complained, clapping him hard on the back. "Stop sulking and look where we are. This is *heaven*."

Heaven, or Mugs 'n' Jugs, a triple X strip club on Route 47 that promised Live! Nude! Girls! and failed to card even its most obvious underage patrons. Adam had made the traditional pilgrimage out here for his sixteenth birthday, but hadn't been back since.

Now he remembered why. Sure, a few of the girls were hot, parading across the stage in their barely-there costumes, this one a tiger-lady, that one a vampiress, all of them flashing the same *fuck me* look at their loser clientele. But once you tore your eyes away from all that bare skin, you couldn't help but notice all the depressing details: the worn-out speaker system, piping the same five songs on a maddening continuous loop; the overpriced drinks and underpaid waitresses; the middle-aged businessmen who'd snuck away from their dreary lives to spend a few hours pretending that the strippers were performing just for them, that their bored *come hither* expressions were more than just business.

"Why'd you drag me here?" he complained, shouting to be heard over the loud techno beat. "I thought we were just going to shoot some pool."

"What are you complaining about?" the center asked. "Look around you and tell me this isn't better than pool." He looked up at the waitress, who'd stopped at their table to clear their drinks, and was leaning so low across Adam that her bare midriff brushed his shoulder. "Hey, baby," the center leered, and pointed toward the stage. "Why aren't you up there with the rest of the hotties?"

Adam cringed, but thankfully, the waitress ignored the idiot. She turned to Adam instead. He cringed again.

"Hey, sweetie, why so glum?" she asked, stroking her finger across his jawline. "Don't see anything you like?"

Adam took a deep breath, almost choking on the heady mix of smoke and cheap perfume.

"It's not that," he stuttered. "I'm . . . uh . . ."

"Distracted," the waitress guessed. She slapped a small glass down on the table and poured him a shot. "It's a girl, isn't it?"

"No, it's—" How to answer that? He couldn't get his mind off a girl, yes, but which girl? The one he wanted to kiss, or the one he wanted to throttle?

"It's always a girl," the waitress said knowingly. She poured a second shot, then lifted the glass herself. "She's not worth it, kid. You're too young for that face." She squeezed his cheeks together and gave his face a gentle shake, like a grandmother doting on her angelic little boy. Then, in a decidedly un-grandmotherly move, she wrapped his fingers around his glass, clinking hers against it.

"To forgetting," she toasted, and downed the shot. She looked at him expectantly, and so he tipped his head back and dumped the drink into his mouth, trying not to choke as the cheap tequila lit a fire down his throat.

"You're still frowning, kid."

"I—"

"Let's try this." And the waitress put down her tray, grabbed his face with both hands, pulled it toward hers, and kissed him. Hard. Fast. Wet. Sloppy. And incredible.

She pulled away, and Adam just gaped at her, dazed, as the warm tequila buzz spread through his body and the cheers and hoots of his buddies beat dimly against his ears.

"There, that should do it," she said, using her thumb to wipe away a lingering smudge of lipstick on his lips, just as his mother had done when he was a child. "Now enjoy the show."

"*That* was fucking unbelievable," the center said in a low voice.

"You are officially the luckiest guy in the world," the point guard added, back from his failed trip to the edge of the stage.

Adam tried to smile as his buddies clapped him on the back and roared with approval. A couple years ago, this whole scene would have been a dream come true. But he wasn't that guy anymore. Not even a hot kiss from a hot, half-naked woman could change that. The kiss just made things worse; he was ashamed to be there, because he knew *Beth* would be ashamed, if she ever found out—if she even cared.

"Woo-hoo, baby!" the center cried, waving a fistful of cash at the blond bombshell who was sliding up and down a metal pole a few feet away. "Bring it on!"

Adam sighed and closed his eyes. If he couldn't leave, he could at least pretend he was somewhere else, with someone else. He'd gotten good at pretending, lately; real life was so much easier to handle when you just ignored it.

Kaia tipped back her head to catch the last few drops of liquid in the glass, then sucked in an ice cube. She needed something bitingly cool to distract her. Sitting this close to Reed, with a table keeping their bodies apart, was driving her crazy.

She'd met him at Guido's as planned, and they were sharing a free pizza before making their escape. She of course hadn't mentioned anything about her unplanned pit stop on the way. Not because he would have had any right to know, she reminded herself, and certainly not because she felt guilty—it just wasn't worth the trouble. She'd met Powell at his apartment and used his desperation as leverage to achieve an unprecedented goal: open windows. Usually obsessively paranoid about keeping every moment of their encounter shut off from the public view, Powell had let himself be cajoled into pulling up the blinds, giving Kaia her first ever look at the view from his apartment. It was, as she'd expected, just as squalid as the apartment itself. Then came the true triumph: persuading Powell to open the sliding-glass door at the back of his bungalow and actually take her outside, if you could count a five-by-five-foot fenced-in square of weeds and gravel as "outside."

They had stood for a moment at the threshold gazing out at the claustrophobic patch as if it were the Garden of Eden and they were considering a rebellious return, and then Powell had taken her hand and led her into the not-so-great outdoors. It was dirty and uncomfortable, and something about the fresh air or the fear of discovery had made Powell more insatiable than usual, nearly endangering her twenty minutes-and-out plan, but it had been well worth it. She'd talked him into breaking his own rules, just for the privilege of being with her, and there was nothing sweeter than that. Or at least, that's how she had felt until Reed had greeted her with a kiss, fully unaware that he was getting used goods, and her victory began to feel unsettlingly hollow.

"You miss it? Home?" Reed asked, nibbling on a piece of crust.

Kaia opened her mouth to give Reed her well-rehearsed speech on the wonders of Manhattan, from the sample sales and the galleries to the way the skyscrapers sliced into the sky on a clear winter morning, from sneaking into club openings and showing up on "Page Six," to meeting up at dawn for a goat cheese omelet and bread fresh from the farmers' market before sneaking home to bed. But she stopped before she said anything.

"I don't know," she admitted—and it was the first time she'd let herself think it, much less speak it aloud. "Sometimes I miss it—I hate it here. But . . . I hated it there, too."

Another guy might have seized the moment to put on the fake sympathy, giving her a "comforting" pat on the thigh and maybe letting his hand rest there a bit too long.

Reed simply asked, "Why?"

"I don't know." And, with another guy, she would have taken this as her cue to heave a calculated sigh, designed to elicit pity or to highlight her ample, heaving chest. Instead, a small, light shiver of air escaped her as her body sagged with the energy of wondering: What was wrong with her life? "There was my mother. Total bitch. And my—I guess you'd call them my friends." She laughed harshly at the thought. "But that wasn't it. I just . . ."

Reed took her hand—and she knew it wasn't in sympathy or empathy, but out of a desperate need to touch her, because she felt it too.

"I didn't fit there. Not that I fit here," she added, laughing bitterly.

"Know what you mean," Reed said quietly, shaking his head. "But what can you do?"

Kaia didn't say anything, just pressed his hand tightly to her lips. She could never say it out loud, but she knew that, bizarrely, she did fit somewhere. Here, with him. And at least there was some comfort in that.

"Are we having a good time yet?" Harper asked snidely, wrinkling her nose after sipping a whiskey sour that tasted more like fermented lemonade. Kane had promised her a night to remember at an exclusive underground after-hours lounge at the outskirts of town. He'd failed to mention that by "exclusive" he meant "restricted to those qualified for membership in the AARP"; "after hours," on the other hand, apparently meant "after the early bird special."

"How was I supposed to know that tonight was bingo night?" he protested.

Harper stifled a laugh and glanced around. True, no one was actually playing bingo—but with half the population of Grace's senior citizens clinking glasses of stale Scotch and swapping sob stories about hip replacements and burst bunions, it seemed only a matter of time. Apparently, once a month the owner let his father use the lounge for his lodge meetings. Harper and Kane had had to sweet-talk their way in, just for the privilege of listening to the Elks, or Buffalo, or whatever they were, reminisce about the war and complain about how their children never came to visit.

It wasn't quite the pick-me-up they'd had in mind.

"So, let's hear it, Grace—what can I do to turn that frown upside down?" Kane downed his drink in one shot and rested his chin on his hands, as if overwhelmingly eager to hear her response.

"As if you could help," Harper said, but without bitterness. They'd known each other too long for her to put up a brave front—or to think that confiding in Kane would yield anything but apathy with a side of scorn. "I don't want to talk about it."

"Don't want to talk about *him,* you mean," Kane said, with a knowing smirk. "Fine, then. What about her?"

"Her who?"

"The Siamese twin from whom you seem to have had a miracle separation? Miranda—who else? Ten years, the two of you are joined at the hip, and then suddenly, in your darkest hour, she's nowhere to be found? Makes no sense," Kane complained, shaking his head. "Not unless there's something I don't know. And you know how much I hate to be in the dark."

"Get used to it," Harper snarled. "There's a lot you don't know." She could tell Kane all about Miranda's massive crush—after all, she had no reason to keep Miranda's secret when her own were spread all over school. But Harper couldn't bring herself to do it, knowing that if there was even a prayer of fixing things—and she had to believe there was—she should keep her mouth shut.

"I can't imagine that Ms. Stevens would have been so disgusted by your treatment of Adam that she would have walked away," Kane mused. "After all, she's nothing but lovely to me, and my behavior was just as . . . let's say, repulsive? Stealing my best friend's girlfriend and all."

"That's not guilt I hear, is it?" Harper asked in surprise.

Kane cocked his head. "You know me better than that.

It's just honesty. I've been telling you for years, Grace, you should just embrace your dark side. You'll have more fun."

"I couldn't be having any less," Harper complained, gesturing toward the speakers that had just begun blasting out some big-band golden oldies.

"No, you must have done something *to* Miranda," Kane continued. He wouldn't stop pushing until he figured it out—but Harper wasn't about to help him along. "And if it's not about Adam, and not about Beth, it must be something else. *Someone* else—"

"May I have this dance, madam?"

Harper looked up to face a balding, pockmarked man stooped over their table and extending a liver-spot-sprinkled hand in her direction. Under other circumstances, she might have—oh, who was she kidding, *would* have—declined. But if it gave her an escape from this conversation . . .

"I'd be honored," Harper said, taking his trembling hand and rising from the table.

Kane's grin widened, and he gave her a jaunty little wave. "Have fun, Grace. Just keep those hands where I can see them. . . ."

The old man danced her away from the table, away from Kane and his nagging questions, and waltzed her across the lounge, proving to be surprisingly nimble. As soon as the song ended, another lodge member hobbled over to take his place. By the time every little old man in the place—at least the ones still mobile enough to shuffle along without a walker—had taken his turn, Kane was slouched on the table, his breathing heavy and his eyes half closed, the Miranda issue forgotten.

"Have fun?" he slurred, without lifting his head from the table.

"Actually, yes." She hadn't even minded when one of the men grabbed her ass. It was nice to be an object of desire again, even among the Viagra demographic.

"Told you so," Kane mumbled, half to himself. "Promised you a night to remember."

But Harper had done enough remembering for a while. That had been the best part about dancing in the darkness in the palsied arms of a stranger: It became almost possible to forget.

He had to congratulate himself. He'd made it through the evening without allowing his emotions to leak through, his anger to explode. She had no idea that he'd seen her, with *him*.

Hidden in the shadows, he'd watched her betray him. Even then, he couldn't help but admire her delicate porcelain skin, pale as ivory against her ink-black hair. She moved like a dancer, every swish of her arm and tilt of her head graceful and deliberate, almost as if she knew he was watching, and was performing just for him. And for a moment, he'd imagined that his hands followed hers, trailing their way across her soft, creamy skin.

But it was another man who took her hand in his. A stolen hand, a stolen touch—there should be punishment for taking something that doesn't belong to you, he thought now. There should be punishment for giving it away, as she did, to another.

He could have turned away—he'd seen enough to know the truth. But he had stayed, waited, watched. She could play with all the men she wanted, but in the end, no one knew her like he did. No one but him knew the way she moved when she thought no one was watching.

The time they spent together was tainted now by what she'd done. But when he watched her in the darkness, that was pure. She could lie to him all she wanted, but she couldn't avoid the truth: She belonged to him.

Apparently, she just needed a reminder.

# chapter

## 5

*"Jump! Jump! Rebound!*
   *Make the shot!*
   *Number 8 is hot! Hot! Hot!"*
The cheerleaders flashed their pom poms, soared through the air, and led the crowd in a thundering chorus, hundreds of fans all chanting his name.
   *"We're the team*
   *That's sure to win,*
   *'Cause MORGAN always gets it in!*
   *Morgan!*
   *Morgan!*
   *Morgan!"*
What a rush.

Number 8, Adam Morgan, dribbled up court, his heart pounding, his feet slamming into the boards. He could feel the Weston Wolves closing in behind him, longing to pounce, but he was faster. Stronger. Better.

After weeks of playing like shit, it had all fallen into

place, now, in this moment. Adam could feel his body shift into motion, a seamless connection between legs, hands, ball, net; instinct took over, driving everything from his mind but the harsh *crack* of the ball against the floor and the stinging *slap* as it rebounded against his cupped palm. He pushed himself forward, outpacing the Wolves and breaking free to a wide-open court, until, finally, he could feel this was his moment; it was a certainty that went beyond reason.

He stopped, scooped up the ball, lifted it above his head, ready to send it flying, and then, just as the ball tipped off his fingertips at the perfect angle—

A shove. Hard, from behind. Knocking Adam off balance.

And the ball bounced off the rim.

Adam barely registered what happened next: the outraged cries of his teammates, the crowd calling foul, the ref calling nothing. All he saw was his ball rolling off the rim and crashing to the floor, and the red, sweaty, sneering face of the guy who'd pushed him.

Somewhere within him, a voice urged restraint—but it was too late for that. Adam launched himself at the sneering Weston Wolf, sucker punching him in the gut and then, as the Wolf bent over, gasping for breath, kicking his legs out from under him, and knocking him to the floor.

And that was all it took.

The Wolves rushed the court to defend their man, and the Haven High Coyotes charged in to make it an even fight. Soon the court was filled with the grunts and thuds of a dozen basketball players punching and clawing one another—and the angry hoots of the crowd, cheering them on.

After all, who doesn't like a little blood with their sport?

The refs blew their whistles and the coaches rushed in to pull their players away, but they couldn't fight the chaos. And, somehow, in the confusion, after knocking one Wolf flat on his ass and barely avoiding the wrong end of a large fist, Adam found himself face-to-face with the true enemy.

Kane grinned at Adam, perhaps forgetting himself in the heat of battle. His usually perfect hair was drenched with sweat and plastered to his forehead, his eyes were wild, and a small trail of blood trickled down his face from a scratch along his temple. He smiled. And Adam exploded.

Lunging at Kane, he grabbed his old friend around the neck, pushed him against the floor, and punched him hard, in the face, where it would hurt the most, bruising his cartilage and his vanity. Adam wanted to keep punching, to feel the rhythm of Kane's head slamming against the floor as if it were the ball, even while Kane gave up fighting back and curled up tight, waiting for it to end. And, simultaneously exhilarated and disgusted by the unfamiliar bloodlust, he might have done it—but they pulled Adam off and threw him to the sidelines with the rest of his team.

He'd gotten only that first punch. Maybe, in the confusion, no one had noticed Adam turning his back on the rivals, attacking his own teammate instead. Or if someone had noticed, hopefully it would be written off as a tragic but inescapable episode of friendly fire for which no one need be held accountable.

Whatever happened next, it would be worth it for the satisfaction he'd received from the sound of Kane's head smacking against the floor and the rush of power coursing through him like a drug.

Adam wouldn't soon forget it.

And, he knew, neither would Kane.

The letters were red, almost glowing against the shiny black paint of the freshly washed BMW.

*Red like blood,* Kaia thought, shivering, even as she berated herself for reacting, determined not to give him—and whoever it was, it must be a him—the satisfaction.

She looked up and down the massive driveway. There was no one in sight, but that didn't mean no one was watching. The floodlights cast shadows across the grounds that seemed to flicker and shudder at the corner of her eye.

*You're imagining things,* she told herself. But she hadn't imagined the sound of breaking glass that had drawn her outside. And she hadn't imagined her car—the front window broken, and those letters spray-painted across its side. The floodlights cast it in a spotlight, and though she knew she should hurry inside, she couldn't turn away.

She'd take it to the garage in the morning, she decided, forcing herself to think analytically, in hopes that would stop the trembling. She'd go early so the maids wouldn't see it and report back to her father. If she told Daddy Dearest that there'd been a flat tire, he would pay as much as she asked, and she could tack on an extra hundred to ensure the mechanic would keep his mouth shut—no reason to spread her humiliation across town.

Kaia whipped her head to the left, suddenly certain she'd glimpsed a pale face peering out from the shadows. But there was no one there. She backed away from the car, edged toward her house, slipped inside, and locked the door. Then she entered in the code for her father's state-of-the-art alarm system, the one she'd always mocked him for buying when there was nothing around for miles but the occasional coyote. Even if some lunatic did stumble upon Chez Sellers and set off the howling alarm, who would be around to hear it?

She decided it was probably best not to dwell on the emptiness outside, or the miles separating her from Grace's lackluster police department, which was largely staffed by local, part-time volunteers and closed up shop at five P.M. Instead, Kaia curled up on the couch, tucked a cashmere throw around her shoulders, and flipped on the TV. She turned up the volume, hoping to drown out the silence that seemed to hold far too many soft, rustling noises that could be footsteps, or a hand brushing up against the window.

*Forget it,* she told herself, peering out the window into the night. *You're being paranoid.*

But it wasn't paranoia if someone was really out to get you, right? And someone must be. Why else would he have scarred the car with his angry red scrawl, branding her with the word that kept pounding in her ears no matter how much she raised the TV volume.

*WHORE.*

Before Harper had trashed their friendship, Miranda had had plenty of opportunities to see Kane. Now, most of the time, her only hope was a glimpse of him in the halls or across the cafeteria. Basketball games, however, provided a two-hour stretch of uninterrupted Kane-gazing, which almost made the endless boredom and inevitable postgame headache worth it.

Tonight she was wishing for boredom. Most of the crowd seemed invigorated by the brawl, but Miranda still felt sick at the thought of Kane lying on the court, bloodied and pale. He'd pulled himself up, limped over to the bench, and sat down next to the other players penalized for the fight—he was obviously intact, she reassured herself. But still she worried, mostly about whether she'd be able to push through the crowd of bimbos at the end of the game and see for herself that he was safe and whole.

Maybe Kane dreaded the bimbos as much as she did, because ten minutes before the end of the final quarter, he quietly slipped off toward the locker room. He would probably change quickly and head for the parking lot, Miranda realized, in hopes of avoiding the crowd. She didn't let herself wonder whether he might want to avoid her, too—at this point, hesitation would just make her chicken out.

She caught up with him in the parking lot, limping toward his car.

"Kane!" she called, not quite loudly enough for him to hear. There was still time to walk away, before she risked humiliation.

But not enough time, because he'd heard her, after all.

"Stevens!" He waved and, even from a distance, she could see him wince. He brought his arm down and cradled it against his side. She trotted over, and he gave her a weak smile. Without thinking, she touched his face gently, where a large, purplish bruise had bloomed just under his eye.

"You should see the other guy," he said ruefully.

Miranda usually agonized over every word she said to Kane, striving for the perfect combination of confidence, solicitation, and flirtatious banter. But now she didn't stop to think, or disguise her concern behind her wit. "Look what they did to you," she murmured.

"It's not so bad."

"You obviously haven't looked in a mirror yet," she said, wrapping an arm around his waist. He leaned against her, and she forced herself to keep breathing. "Come on, I'm helping you to your car."

"I'm fine, I swear."

"Humor me." They made it to the Camaro, and Kane climbed into the front seat, then looked up at her expectantly. "Well?"

"What?"

"Aren't you coming? Or is your nursing shift over for the night?"

Her heart fluttering, Miranda went around to the passenger seat and closed the door behind her. By the light of the dashboard, she could see that his face wasn't cut up as badly as she'd thought, but it still looked plenty painful. She pulled a water bottle out of her bag and dug around for a tissue. Wetting it, she began dabbing away some of the dried blood dotting his face. He squirmed away as she held the damp tissue against a cut at the edge of his lip.

"Don't be a baby," she chided him. "This'll help."

"You're good at this," he said softly.

"What? Washing faces?"

"Making people feel better."

Miranda blushed, and all her self-consciousness flooded

back. "Just call me Florence Nightingale," she said wryly.

Her hand still pressed lightly against his lips. Suddenly, Kane mirrored the gesture, bringing his hand to her face and tipping her chin so they were staring into each other's eyes. "Don't joke," he insisted. The infamous Kane Geary smirk was nowhere to be seen. "I mean it. Thank you."

She couldn't allow herself to be honest, and she didn't want to spoil the moment by saying something funny. So she said nothing, and neither did he. They faced each other in silence, their faces illuminated by only the glowing dashboard and the flashing lights of passing cars pulling out of the lot.

*Does he know what I'm thinking?* she asked herself as she stared at his bruised face and his swollen lips, wishing that this was about more than his gratitude. The soft, almost glazed look in his eyes made it seem almost possible. And he still hadn't taken his hand away from her face. *Does he finally see me?* she wondered. *Does he finally get it?*

And then, as if there'd been a signal that only he could hear, Kane moved away and turned the key in the ignition. "I'm headed home," he said brusquely. "Where can I drop you?"

She could go along with him, staring out the window and praying that when he stopped the car they would regain that moment of honest intimacy. Maybe things would even go further, and she'd have more than just a long gaze and a lingering touch to dream about tonight. But the moment of decision had obviously passed—and he'd decided no. Why torture herself with something that wasn't going to happen?

"Actually, I drove tonight," Miranda said, opening the

car door. "So I guess you're on your own. If you think you can make it."

Kane grinned. "I'm fine, Doctor. Stop worrying." He reached for her hand and brought it to his lips in a mock-gallant gesture. Miranda hoped he wouldn't notice her trembling. "Many thanks for your services tonight."

"It was nothing," Miranda said, and she jumped out of the car before he could read the lie on her face.

Beth stared hatefully at the blinking cursor on her computer screen, the only thing marring the white wasteland of her empty document. Maybe if she stared long enough, she thought, the words would write themselves, and she could just give up and go to bed.

She'd already wasted an hour meditating on "Why Education Is Important," finding it to easy to get distracted by topics such as "Why the Principal Thinks This Is a Good Topic," "What the Odds Are This Speech Will Put the Governor to Sleep," and "How I Can Keep Harper from Ruining My Life—Again."

Beth still couldn't quite believe that Harper was going to enter, despite her threats. She could barely be bothered to do her homework most days, so how likely was it that she'd put in a nonrequired show of academic effort and produce a whole speech? But Beth had to assume that she'd go through with it, if only because Harper's desire to destroy her had so far proved unbounded. It didn't seem fair; without Harper in the race, Beth's win would have been a sure thing.

*I deserve this,* she told herself. She worked harder than anyone at Haven High. The rest of them were complacent, contented with their narrow, small-town lives—it was only Beth who wanted more.

She opened her Web browser and clicked back to the Web site she'd come across of award-winning essays on every topic. According to the description at the top of the page, it was supposed to serve as an inspiration for students in her position, but Beth knew what it was *really* for. She'd always known sites like this one were out there, she just never thought she'd be visiting one herself.

But her mind was so clogged with bitterness that she couldn't string two sentences together, much less compose a speech. And here they were, dozens of them—all better than anything she could have come up with, even on her best day. She could just highlight the text, cut and paste, change a few words here and there . . .

It would be wrong, not to mention risky and totally beneath her—she was supposed to be someone who, unlike Harper, actually had principles.

It would be wrong, she repeated to herself.

But it would also work.

"What do you want?"

At the sound of Miranda's voice, Harper was momentarily stunned into silence. "I . . . uh . . . didn't expect you to actually pick up." Waiting for Miranda to screen her call, then leaving a plaintive voice mail that would inevitably go unreturned had become a nightly routine for Harper. This was an unexpected break in the pattern, and now that she had an opening, she had no idea what she actually wanted to say.

"I guess it's a night of surprises," Miranda replied, almost dreamily.

"What?"

"I'm just ... tonight was ... let's just say you caught me in a good mood. Your lucky day. So what do you want?"

Harper wasn't sure whether she wanted to apologize yet again, or to accuse Miranda of having spread the gossip flyer and force an admission that now the two of them were even. So instead, she stalled for time. "Just to talk," she said slowly. "Just to see what's up with you."

"Same old, same old." Miranda's voice wasn't overly friendly, but it lacked that icy sheen she usually adopted when forced to talk to Harper. Maybe there was hope after all.

Carpe diem, right?

"Look, Miranda, I'm sorry," Harper said quickly, trying to spit out as many words as she could before Miranda cut her off. "I'm so sorry, you have to understand that I would never want to hurt you, or our friendship, and you know how important Adam is—was—but he wasn't more important than you—"

"Whatever," Miranda muttered.

Harper's fingers tightened around the phone. "No, really—I know you think I screwed you, but I *didn't*. I swear, if I had thought there was a chance in hell that something would happen between you and Kane—"

"Stop."

"But you need to know that—"

"Just stop." And it was back, that flat, affectless tone that belied the years of friendship between them. Whatever opening had briefly existed, it had just slammed shut. "I don't need to hear any more about how I'm not good enough for him. I already know what you think."

"Of course it's not what I think," Harper protested. "It's Kane, it's—"

"No, it's *you*. Maybe if you'd actually, oh, I don't know, *helped* me, rather than stabbed me in the back . . ."

Her voice trailed off, and for a moment there was nothing but the sound of loud breathing on both ends of the line. "Is that why you did it?" Harper asked softly. "It's really all about Kane?"

"Did what?"

"I know it was you," Harper said, trying to keep a lid on her emotions. If Miranda wanted to handle this like they were strangers, Harper would find the strength to do so.

"Is this some kind of riddle?"

"Beth couldn't have done it on her own," Harper continued. "There were things on there that no one else knew."

"So?"

"So it was you. God, Rand, teaming up with *her*? Do you really hate me that much?"

There was a long pause. "Maybe."

"Just because I didn't help you get Kane?" Harper asked incredulously.

Miranda sighed. "It's not Kane . . . not just Kane." She no longer sounded angry, or bitter, just tired. "It's you. I kept making excuses for you. Whenever anyone called you a heartless bitch, or a slut—"

As always, Harper jerked at the sound of the word. She hated the way it sounded—especially on Miranda's lips.

"I'd always say, 'Oh no, you don't know what you're talking about. *You* don't know her like *I* know her.' So congratulations," she said sarcastically, "you fooled me. But now I'm done. I'm out."

"Just like that?" Harper asked, the taste of bile rising in the back of her throat. "I'm a bitch, you're a saint, and now Saint Miranda's *'out'*?"

"That's not—well, yes."

"That's bullshit, Rand, and you know it." Harper collapsed onto her bed, staring up at the ceiling. Her voice was cold enough that Miranda would never suspect there were tears streaming down her face, or that she'd tugged a blanket over her head as if to shut out the world. "You can act like you're better than me, but we both know the truth: You're jealous."

Miranda rolled her eyes. "Of you? Right."

"Yes. *Right.*" Harper hated herself for saying it, but Miranda wasn't the only one who could be cruel. "You hate that I get all the attention and you just have to tag along after me. You're just using this as an excuse to get away because you think that without me around, you might actually be *someone.*"

"So what?"

"So think again." Harper knew she should stop—even if apologies wouldn't work, time might, if she just shut up. But it didn't matter what she wanted; her hand was glued to the phone. "At least with me, people knew who you were. You had friends. You had a life. Without me? You've got nothing." *It's almost too late,* she warned herself, but she couldn't stop. "You *are* nothing."

Harper's voice broke on the last word, but when Miranda finally spoke, she sounded perfectly composed.

"Maybe you're right," she said slowly, just before hanging up. "But I'd rather be nothing than be your friend."

Kaia almost ignored the doorbell—but that would mean she had let him win, right? Whoever he was out there who wanted to terrify her would have accomplished his goal. And Kaia refused to play that game.

"I hoped you'd be here," Reed said when she opened the door.

Hoped, or knew?

"What are you doing here?" Reed almost never showed up at her house. It wasn't his style. Instead, she would call him and they'd meet on some neutral territory. Was it possible he'd come tonight to check up on his handiwork, and see whether she'd fallen apart?

It couldn't be him, she told herself. Not Reed, the one person out here she'd grown to trust. Except—

*How much do you really know about him?*

Nothing.

Enough.

"Got tired of admiring you from afar," Reed said, smiling. "Figured it was time you met your secret admirer."

Alarmed, Kaia took a step back.

"Hey, it was just a joke," he said softly, taking her hands in his. "I just wanted to see you, that's all. Missed you. What's going on?"

Kaia was glad she'd turned the floodlights off before going inside, so there was no way he could have seen her vandalized car in the darkness. For a second, she considered flicking them back on and telling him everything, but she didn't want him to look at her as a victim. Or maybe she was afraid he wouldn't be surprised.

"Nothing," she said, insisting to herself that it was true. "I'm glad you came."

She forced herself to forget her ridiculous suspicions and forget the fact that the maids were out for the night and her father wasn't due back until tomorrow. And after they shared a long, deep kiss, she was almost able to do it.

Kaia led him out back to the hot tub, tossing him a pair of her father's trunks. Then she ducked into the changing room and slipped into her new bikini, determined not to let some perverted loser ruin her night.

As they let themselves sink into the churning water, Kaia knew she'd made the right decision. This was just what she needed to relax, and remind herself that Reed wasn't a threat.

"Glad I came over?"

Kaia launched herself across the hot tub and floated into Reed's arms. The nearly unbearable heat was even worse with his wet, sticky body pressed up against hers, but Kaia didn't mind. The heat was refreshing—cleansing. "Definitely."

He wrapped himself around her and then sank down farther into the seat, so they were both nearly submerged in the roiling water, with only their faces peeking out into the sharp winter breeze. He tipped his head back. "Look at that," he said reverently.

Kaia followed his gaze. The stars seemed unnaturally bright. One of them, twinkling by the horizon, had a dark, reddish glow. "I wouldn't want to be anywhere else right now," she marveled. Contentment was a new thing for her.

"Good, because you're staying right where you are," he said, turning her around to face him. Her hair floated in a halo around her, and she remembered that when she was a little girl, she had pretended to be a mermaid. She'd always thought she looked most beautiful in the water.

She inhaled deeply, burrowing her face into his neck. The water had washed away the ever-present stench of pot, the lingering grease from his tow truck and his shift at Guido's—he was fresh and clean. Just like new. "I like the way you smell."

"I like *you*." He kissed her, roughly at first, his tongue thrusting into her mouth, tangling itself with hers, their breath loud and hurried in her ear. Then as she nibbled on his lower lip and opened her eyes, he opened his, and their movement slowed, until they were almost frozen, their lips connected, their eyes locked.

"What the hell is going on here?"

Reed flinched and thrust himself away from her, but Kaia didn't refuse to let go. She'd recognize the harsh, patrician voice anywhere—Daddy Dearest was hard to forget. She wasn't about to let him ruin her fun, not tonight. She needed Reed by her side, as a flesh-and-blood reminder that she wasn't alone.

"I should think that's pretty obvious," she quipped, finally looking up. He loomed over them, far enough back to ensure no water would touch his custom-tailored Ermenegildo Zegna suit and Bruno Magli loafers. "What are you doing home?"

"I live here," he reminded her.

It was only technically true. Two or three nights a month he lived there. The rest of the time it was difficult to remember his existence. The maid could have warned her he was due home tonight, Kaia thought in irritation.

No matter—she could be dealt with later. For now, the damage was done.

"What's the problem, Father?" she asked innocently. "I'm just making new friends. Isn't that what you wanted? I thought the whole point of sending me out here was so I could meet some new people. You know, good influences."

She tried to stroke Reed's hair, but he jerked away and pulled out of her grasp.

Her father ignored her, as usual.

"Who are you?" he asked, glaring at Reed. "Get off my daughter and out of my Jacuzzi." Reed stumbled to his feet, stepped up onto the wooden deck and, dripping, extended a hand to Keith Sellers.

Mistake.

Kaia's father looked at him as he might a wet, stinky dog who'd tried to rub up against the leg of his $1,200 pants.

"Reed Sawyer, sir," Reed said, dropping his hand when it became obvious no one was going to shake it.

"I know you, don't I?"

"He works at the garage down on Main Street," Kaia said brightly. "You probably saw him there when you took the Jag in for service."

Now Keith Sellers looked as if the wet dog had *peed* on his $1,200 pants.

"Or maybe he delivered your pizza," Kaia added helpfully, just to dig the knife in a little deeper. She knew very well that Keith Sellers *never* ordered pizza, even when he wasn't on his no-carb diet.

Her father heaved a weary sigh.

"What are you doing, Kaia?" he asked, shaking his head. "This is a lot of effort to go to, just to spite me."

"This has nothing to do with you," Kaia snapped. She climbed out of the tub and wrapped a towel around herself, handing one to Reed as well. He took it without looking at her.

"Why else would you be associating with this kind of trash?" Keith Sellers shrugged his shoulders and then strode back toward the house. On his way, he hit the lights, dropping them into darkness. Kaia could no longer see Reed's face—or guess what he might be thinking. "Get him out of here, Kaia," he called back to her, in a voice she knew better than to disobey. "I know you'll do whatever you want—but you're not doing it in my house."

It was so pathetic when he actually tried to act parental. He was just too out of practice for it to stick.

"Come on," she said, taking Reed's hand and pulling him toward the door. "Let's get out of here."

"I'm going," Reed agreed, pulling his hand away. He rested it firmly on her shoulder. "You stay."

"What? Why?" *Listen to me,* she thought in disgust, *needy and pathetic.* "Who cares what he thinks?" she asked. "I don't."

"I think you do," he said slowly, avoiding her gaze. "And that's the problem."

He walked away, and because she didn't want to seem weak, she didn't follow. She let the towel drop to the floor of the deck and in the darkness groped her way back to the forgiving waters of the hot tub.

*Damn him,* she thought, sinking in. Damn him for his pride, or stubbornness, or whatever had made him leave.

And damn her father. He'd been absent most of her life—was *still* absent—and despite the fact that she never asked anything of him, he kept taking everything that mattered to her. He'd taken her home, her credit cards, her freedom—and now Reed.

He wouldn't be happy until she was left alone, with nothing.

Oh wait—

Mission accomplished.

He didn't go straight to his pickup truck, but instead wandered off into the darkness, telling himself he was exploring the grounds—but the truth was, he couldn't bring himself to leave. He stopped after a few minutes, realizing that he had a perfect view of the back deck hot tub, Kaia's figure illuminated in the darkness. She was so beautiful, he couldn't bring himself to turn away. Especially since it was becoming clear that the two of them didn't belong together, not in the real world. Out here, watching, he could forget all that and just appreciate her. He could remember the way she'd felt in his arms, and forget that she was likely just playing him, stringing him along for her own purposes.

Reed sighed, resisting the urge to light up. He needed something to take the edge off. Kaia was like a drug that made everything seem too real. It was as if he lived the rest of his life in black and white. With Kaia, the world wasn't just brighter—it was blinding Technicolor.

And it was exhausting.

Reed spent most of his life hanging on the sidelines. It was his natural place, just as waiting and watching was his

"This is a very quite serious charge, Ms. Grace." Jack Powell frowned sternly at her, and ran a hand through his floppy brown hair. "Do you have any evidence to back up these claims?"

Other than absolute certainty in the pit of her stomach? Other than nearly explicit—but undocumented—admissions from both suspects? Uh . . .

"No," she admitted. "I was hoping you could handle that. Now that you know what you're looking for."

"And why come to me with this information? Why not the vice principal, or someone else in the administration?"

"Well, I figure they must have used the newspaper equipment to print the flyer, and you *are* the sponsor. It seemed like your department." Harper hoped it sounded convincing. She wasn't about to admit that when you're turning in your former best friend for stabbing you in the back, it's more palatable to do so with the hottest teacher natural state. But with Kaia he found himself acting, rather than reacting, his normally placid mind consumed with questions: Why did she want him? Why did he want her? How would things end, and when?

Maybe it had been a mistake to get involved at all.

Reed decided to light up after all, and inhaled deeply, relishing the heat that spread through his lungs. Being with Kaia meant being in the center, under the spotlight. And he just wasn't made for that kind of hassle. He lived on the fringes. He didn't *do*. He watched.

in the history of Haven High. Besides, Vice Principal Sorrento had a creepy birthmark on his forehead that had already eaten most of his hair and would surely soon get started on his face. Mr. Powell, on the other hand, could have been Hugh Grant's stunt double—and pretending she was starring in one of those movies where the sassy American falls into bed with the dapper Englishman was almost enough to distract her from the task at hand.

She'd woken up that morning determined to act. Striking back was the best way to keep from obsessing over Miranda's words and what it meant that the one person who knew her best had decided she wasn't worth knowing.

"Beth Manning and Miranda Stevens are two of my best students," Powell said dubiously. "Are you sure—"

"It was them, Mr. Powell. I'm positive. Just look into it—you'll see I was right."

For a moment, Harper pictured how Miranda's face would look when she got summoned to the vice principal's office to receive her punishment, sure to be especially harsh under the new "no-tolerance" regime. But she pushed the image out of her mind.

Miranda had no regrets, right?

Fine. Good. Then neither would she.

In her backpack, Beth carried: four sharpened Dixon Ticonderoga pencils, and a pale pink pencil sharpener in the shape of a rose. Just in case. One Mead notebook and one matching folder for each class, color coded. A folded-up picture of her twin brothers, stuffed into the front pocket. Two dollars in quarters, for vending machine snacks. A pack of wintergreen Eclipse gum, to help her stay awake in history class, where the teacher had a bad habit of droning on and on about his long-ago European vacation. A Winnie the Pooh wallet she'd gotten on a family trip to Disneyland and had never had the heart to replace. And today, Beth carried two neatly typed, four-page-long speeches on the subject of education, each bound together with a single staple positioned in the upper-left-hand corner.

One speech was eloquent, witty, and succinct, seamlessly shifting back and forth between heartfelt personal anecdotes and powerful generalizations. It was a sure winner.

The second speech was awkward, wordy, and nonsensical, filled with run-on sentences and the occasional misspelling. It was hackneyed and repetitive and made stunningly obvious pronouncements such as, "Without teachers, there could be no schools." It was a loser, from beginning to end.

The first speech was written by a Jane A. Wilder, of Norfolk, New Jersey. The second speech was written by Beth Manning, hastily spit out in the early hours of the morning because, at four A.M., she'd finally given up on sleep and decided that she needed a backup plan in case she decided not to let Jane A. Wilder unknowingly save the day.

As she approached the principal's office, she took both essays out of her bag. There was a box, just inside the door, marked SPEECHES FOR THE GOVERNOR. It was almost empty—but lying on top was one titled "Education: You Break It, You Buy It." By Harper Grace.

Beth resisted the temptation to pull it out of the box and read it—she'd rather not know. And she resisted the even stronger temptation to take it from the box, stuff it in her backpack, and run away.

Instead, she focused on her choice: Do the right thing or do the smart thing.

What good would it do her to be an ethical person if she was stuck practicing her ethics in Grace, California for the rest of her life, earning a junior college degree in food preparation and then working at the diner for the next fifty years until she dropped dead of boredom in the middle of a vat of coleslaw? On the other hand, what good would it be to wow the admissions committee, earning her ticket to a bright and better tomorrow, all the while knowing she was living a life that, in truth, belonged to Jane A. Wilder of Norfolk, New Jersey?

She did what she had to do.

She flipped a coin—and in the flicker of disappointment that shot through her as soon as she saw Abraham Lincoln's stern profile gazing up from the center of her palm, she realized the decision she wanted to make. She ignored the coin, and put one of the speeches back in her bag. The other went into the box.

Right or wrong, it was, in the end, her only choice.

Adam shuffled into the coach's office and slouched down in the uncomfortable metal folding chair, doing his best to avoid the coach's hostile stare. They sat in silence for a moment as Adam waited for the shouting to begin. He'd been waiting all week for the coach to summon him about the big fight and finally dish out his punishment. But that didn't mean he was looking forward to it. And he had no intention of speaking first.

"I assume you know why you're here?" Coach Wilson finally asked.

Adam nodded.

"Instigating a brawl with the whole school watching?" He shook his head. "Not smart."

Adam shrugged.

"The Weston Wolves' point guard broke his nose, and their center will be out for half the season with two broken fingers."

Adam shrugged again.

"Well?" the coach asked, his face reddening the way it did at Saturday morning practice when it was obvious half the team was too hung over to see the ball, much less send it into the basket.

"Well what?" Had there been a question in there somewhere? Adam hadn't been paying much attention. He just wanted to get this over with.

"Well, don't you have anything to say for yourself?"

Adam shook his head.

"Damn it, Morgan!" The coach slammed his palm down on the desk with a thud. "What's wrong with you? When I took over this team, all anyone could talk about was Adam Morgan, how talented he was, what a great team leader he was—and do you know what I found instead?"

Silence.

"I found you. You screw up in practice, you screw up in the games, you're surly, you're unfocused, and on the night you finally start playing to your capacity, you start a damned fight. What's wrong with you?"

Having made it this far into the meeting without saying more than two words, Adam suddenly found the inertia too much to fight.

"I don't know what's going on with you, Morgan, but I don't like it. I've got no use for hotheads."

*Just get to the point,* Adam thought.

"I should probably throw you off the team."

Adam searched himself for shock, despair, or any of the other reactions you'd expect at the thought that basketball, the last good thing in his life, could disappear. But he couldn't find any. He just felt numb. And if getting thrown off the team meant he didn't have to confront Kane's smirk, day in and day out—maybe it would be for the best.

"But I'm not going to. You're too good. I'm giving you one last chance, Morgan. Don't screw it up."

Again, Adam waited for the flood of emotion, relief. It didn't come.

"Don't thank me yet," the coach continued, ignoring the fact that Adam hadn't moved. "You know the administration is cracking down this month. Everyone involved in the fight gets two weeks' detention—except you. As the instigator, in addition to the detentions, you'll be suspended from school for five days."

Suspended, while everyone else, including Kane, got off with detention? That was enough to slice through Adam's apathy.

"Coach, the other guys were all in it, just as much as I was. I *saw* Kane Geary snap that guy's fingers—" It was a lie, but who cared?

"And *I* saw you take Geary down, so I wouldn't be throwing his name around if I were you. At least he had too

much class to come in here and tattle on you like a little baby."

"Class?" All Kane had was the ability to charm any gullible adult who crossed his path. "He had it coming, Coach," Adam protested, rising from his chair. "You don't know him, he's—" But there was nothing he could say, not here. The frustration building, Adam swept his arms in a long, swift arc, knocking the folding chair off balance. It toppled over and skidded across the floor.

"I'd advise you to calm yourself down now, son," the coach warned. Adam breathed heavily through his mouth and resisted the urge to react to that single, offensive word. Son. Only his father had ever called him that, and only when he was drunk and angry—and Adam had been foolish enough to get in his way. "I'm going to forget we had this little chat, Morgan," the coach said, leaning back in his chair. "And when you come back from your suspension, you and I, we can start with a clean slate. I would advise you to use this week to take a serious look at your behavior, and find a way to get it under control. Before you get yourself into some *serious* trouble." He flicked his hand in dismissal. "Now, get out."

And, ever obedient, Adam did as he was told.

Maybe he would follow the coach's advice and spend his week off trying to relax, trying to move on and forget about the wreck Harper, Kane, and Kaia had made out of his life. Maybe he could even accept that Beth wasn't going to forgive him. Maybe he could find a way to live without the constant urge to break something.

Maybe.

Kaia used to struggle with staying awake in school; now, though it seemed like she hadn't slept in days, she arrived every morning feeling like she'd injected a double espresso directly into her bloodstream. She was too aware of every set of eyes that might be tracking her path down the hall.

She stared down at her desk every day in French class, feeling Powell's gaze resting on her from across the room. Reed was nowhere to be found, and yet it felt like he was everywhere, lurking in corners, peering out from behind lockers, sneaking glimpses of her—but disappearing as soon as she sensed his presence.

She'd had her car repainted and washed it three times, but she could still trace her fingers along the ghostly letters. They were too faint to make out, but she knew they were there, hiding under the new coat of paint, for only her to see.

So she spent her days watching and waiting, and her nights lingering in town, wandering the narrow, broken down streets of Grace, preferring to stay away from her empty house and its loud silence. The last three nights she'd gone to a movie at the Starview Theater. The same movie was showing each night—*Clueless*. She didn't like the film very much; as someone intimately familiar with a real-world life of luxury, she didn't have much patience with the movie's shoddy impersonation. But still there was something strangely appealing about sitting alone in the dark, surrounded by strangers, watching a completely predictable life unfold with perfect symmetry on the screen.

Besides, it gave her something to do.

It was ridiculous, Kaia told herself, spinning the combination lock on her locker, all this angst over a one-time thing. It could have been a random act of vandalism—it's not like there weren't enough bored delinquents running loose in this town. There was no reason to think that she'd been a carefully chosen target.

Kaia opened up her locker, and a small envelope fell out. An envelope she'd never seen before, an envelope that couldn't have been slipped in through the vent because her locker had no vent. Just a door, and a lock. And someone out there knew the combination.

She looked up and down the hallway. No one was watching her. They were all absorbed in their own lives. Or so it appeared.

The envelope was small, and light blue. And it was blank. She stuck a nail under the seam and slowly ripped it open, unaware that she was holding her breath.

She pulled out three small pieces of glossy paper. And now she breathed again, harsh and fast. They were photos.

The first, a distance shot of her buying a movie ticket.

The second, framed by her living room window, showing her curled up on the couch, eyes fixed on the TV.

The third, a close-up, her head tipped back against a wooden deck, her hair wet and plastered against her face. Her eyes closed. And there was something else in the frame, a hand, reaching down toward her face, toward the lock of hair that covered her left eyes. Proving that it wasn't a telephoto lens, that someone had been there.

Close enough to touch.

"I didn't do it." Miranda could come up with no strategy other than repeating that over and over, until they believed her.

"Ms. Stevens, we have proof. Mr. Powell found traces

of your file on the newsroom computer." The vice principal nodded in the direction of Jack Powell, who stood
behind his desk, stone-faced and silent. "You were the only
one logged in that morning. But we do suspect you had an
accomplice. Who were you working with?"

"No one," Miranda protested. "I didn't do it." She was
shaking. She and Harper had gotten into plenty of trouble
over the years, but never anything that had landed her here,
squeezed into an uncomfortable chair, facing down the
vice principal and fending off the claustrophobic convic-
tion that the walls of his office were closing in. And she'd
never gotten into trouble without Harper by her side. It
was different, she was quickly discovering, when you were
alone.

"If you tell us who it is, Ms. Stevens, I might consider your cooperation when deciding your punishment. What you've done is very serious, you realize. This
will go on your permanent record. It could affect your
entire future."

Was her loyalty to a girl she barely knew and barely
liked really worth getting into even more trouble? Miranda
didn't know—but she knew she wasn't a rat. Once Beth
found out they'd been caught, she would surely insist on
turning herself in—say what you wanted about Beth, she
at least had principles—but Miranda wasn't about to
make the decision for her, no matter what it cost. She lifted
her head up and crossed her arms in an effort to look
resolute—and to stop herself from trembling.

"I'm sorry. I wish I could help you, but I can't."

"This is a one-shot deal, Stevens. Tell me now, and I can
help you. But once I've decided on your punishment—"

"I'm sorry," she repeated. "I can't."

"Very well, then." He rubbed the large brown birthmark on his forehead, then looked down at his desk and began flipping through a stack of papers, as if to signify that she was no longer worth his time. "A month of detentions, then, starting today."

Miranda got up to leave, doing her best to hold back the tears. *Harper* would never cry in a situation like this. She would just grin at the vice principal, making it clear that nothing he could do or say would affect her in the least. Miranda couldn't manage a smile, but at least she didn't cry.

"Stevens," the vice principal said as she was almost out the door, "you've made a very poor choice here today. I hope, for your sake, you don't look back on this moment and realize it was a huge mistake."

Kane ambushed her right outside the vice principal's office. She'd caught him at his weakest moment, so it seemed only fair to return the favor.

"I have to admit," he said, slipping up from behind her, "I didn't think you had it in you."

Miranda flushed and looked away, one hand flying up, as if on its own, to check that her hair was sufficiently in place. The small gesture was all it took to confirm Kane's suspicions.

"Didn't know I had what in me?" she asked in confusion, smiling widely despite the tears forming at the corner of each eye.

"I think you know what." He jerked his head back toward the office. "What'd they give you? Life without parole? Plus a little community service?"

"A month's detention," she said ruefully. "Wait—you know, and you're not mad?"

"Mad?" Kane grinned at her, delighting in the way the blood all rushed back to her face. Not that there weren't plenty of girls falling all over themselves to have him, but Miranda was different. She'd always been a bit of a riddle, and there was something almost comforting about being able to tuck her neatly into a recognizable category. Something a bit disappointing, as well—she didn't belong with the bimbos. "Why would I be mad?" he asked, stroking his chin in deep thought. "Just because you spread a bunch of embarrassing rumors about me to the whole school?"

She raised her eyebrows as if to say, well . . . *yes.*

"I *was* mad," he allowed. But it had, after all, been such a feeble scheme. And there was almost something endearingly pathetic about Miranda's little attempt to strike back. Like a kitten trying to take down a tiger. "I *was* mad," he repeated, "but it's not a deal breaker." He put an arm around her, the way he had a hundred times over the course of their friendship—except, this time, he noticed the way she brightened up at his touch. "Besides, I'm kind of impressed. It's good to see you raising a little hell."

"I learned from the best," she said teasingly.

"Then you didn't learn enough. *I* know better than to get caught," he boasted.

She ducked her head and giggled. It wasn't a sound that suited her. She wasn't a giggler.

"How *did* you know they caught me, by the way?"

"A master never reveals his secrets," Kane swore. His network of informants depended on his discretion—and his power depended on his access to their information. "Let's just say I have my ways."

"Someday, Kane, you're going to find out you don't know everything," Miranda cautioned him.

"And someday, Stevens, you're going to find out I know even more than you think."

Do the right thing, or do the smart thing?

She couldn't flip a coin this time, not with Miranda facing her, waiting for some kind of answer. Miranda was flushed, and kept smiling and staring off into space, as if her brush with the vice principal had completely unhinged her.

"I'd never ask you to turn yourself in," Miranda said again. "I just thought you should know what was going on."

"And they didn't mention me at *all*?" Beth asked. She felt guilty for even considering weaseling out of responsibility, but she'd never been in trouble before, and the prospect of getting caught terrified her. They were huddled over a small table in the library, just across from the shelf of college guides—a vivid reminder of how much Beth stood to lose.

*Maybe you should have thought of that* before *you broke the rules,* a voice in her head suggested.

"No," Miranda confirmed. "They know there's someone else, but they have no idea who it is."

"A month of detentions . . ." Beth couldn't imagine it. She'd never even had one.

And it wasn't just the fear of spoiling her record—her *permanent* record—that stopped her. She worked at the diner after school. On off days she babysat for her little brothers and bounced between countless application-padding extracurriculars. She *couldn't* spend a month in detention; it would ruin everything.

"Do you *want* me to turn myself in?" Beth asked, knowing already that the ironclad rules of the teen honor code would force Miranda to say no, regardless of the truth.

"No, of course not. I mean, unless you . . ."

"I could," Beth offered. "I mean, I would, if you wanted me to. Of course."

"Oh, I know you would, of course."

"But, you know, if you don't really think it would change anything . . . ," Beth hedged.

"No, I guess . . . no reason for us both to go down, right?" Miranda said weakly. "I mean, it seems sort of silly, for you to just—out of solidarity, or something."

"But if you wanted me to—"

"No, only if *you* wanted to—"

She deserved that month of detentions, every bit as much as Miranda. But then—what was the difference?

Did she *deserve* for her boyfriend to cheat on her? Did she deserve to bomb the SATs after all her studying? To cry herself to sleep every night? To be screwed over by Adam, by Harper, by Kane, to be left alone? What had she ever done to deserve any of that?

But what had Miranda done, either, other than come along for the ride?

She opened her mouth, intending to say one thing—and then said another thing entirely.

"Okay, I guess I'll keep quiet," she told Miranda, who gave her a thin smile. "Thank you."

Beth had always thought of herself as someone who did the right thing, but now she knew the truth. She only did the right thing when it didn't cost her anything. She opened her mouth to take it back, but Miranda was already standing up and walking away. Not that it mattered: Beth didn't have the nerve, even if the alternative meant hating herself.

*I'll make it up to you,* she promised Miranda silently. *Somehow.*

Kaia didn't know he was there until he'd crept up behind her and laid a hand on her shoulder. She almost knocked over her coffee when she whirled around and realized he had approached her in a public place, in a coffee shop, where anyone could see. Powell was on permanent orange alert at the possibility of anyone seeing them together, and if he'd elected to throw his obsessive caution to the wind, it could mean only one thing: He was losing it.

"How did you know I was here?" she asked, wondering if he'd been following her.

"I needed to see you," Powell said, ignoring the question. He wrapped his fingers tightly around her forearm and pulled her toward a secluded corner of the deserted coffee shop. She settled into an overstuffed armchair, but he stayed standing, hovering nervously behind her.

"Sit down," she hissed, disgusted. Where was the cool British charmer she'd pursued, the one with the icy glare and the cocky certainty that nothing mattered but what he wanted? "It'll be bad enough if anyone sees us together, but if they see you fluttering around me like a nervous boyfriend—just *sit down.*" She pointed to a chair across from her close enough that they could talk without being overheard, and far enough that he wouldn't be tempted to touch her, even if he'd truly become unhinged.

"So? What is it?" she asked, when he'd finally sat down and a minute had passed in silence. "What do you want?"

"What are you doing?" he asked, almost sorrowfully.

"What am *I* doing?" She arched an eyebrow. "Look where we are. What are *you* doing?"

"You won't return my calls. I needed to see you."

"I've been busy."

He let loose a harsh chuckle. "Busy? In this town? No such thing. No, I can guess what you've been doing."

"And what's that supposed to mean?"

"You've been with *him,* haven't you?"

"You've been watching me?" she said, pretending the realization came as a surprise.

"Of course not." He laughed, a few bitter barks of noise that contained no humor. "I've got better things to do with my time."

He seemed so honestly disdainful of the idea that she almost believed him; but then, if he hadn't been watching her, why the righteous anger? How could he be so sure?

"It's all over town, dearest. You may have some discretion, but your gutter-rat, I'm afraid . . ."

Reed wouldn't have spread anything around, he wasn't the type. But how could she be so certain, she asked herself, about a guy she'd just met? What made her so willing to trust the pizza delivery boy who drove around in a pickup truck, smoked mountains of pot, and never answered any of her questions?

"Let's say, for the sake of argument, that you're right. Let's say I was . . ."

"Cheating on me," Powell supplied helpfully. It was an odd choice of words, since cheating implied a relationship. And whatever they had—an agreement, an unwritten contract, a mutual disregard—it wasn't a relationship.

It was sex, nothing else.

"Whatever," she said, throwing up her hands in supplication. "Let's say you're right. What now?"

He looked surprised—maybe by her unruffled expression, which, she hoped, made it painfully clear that she didn't care what happened next.

"Now? Now you stop seeing him," he ordered. "We agreed—you want this, you want me, you can't have anyone else."

"Fine." Kaia shrugged.

"Fine?" He raised his eyebrows. Maybe he'd been expecting more of a fight. "You'll stop seeing him, then?"

"No." Did she have to spell it out? "I'll stop seeing *you*." She finished her iced coffee in a single gulp and stood up. "It's been fun, Jack. See you around."

"Where do you think you're going?" he growled, grabbing her arm roughly to pull her back down. She shrugged him off. "You think you can just walk away?"

"Pretty much."

"That's not how it works, Kaia. You want to be very careful about what you choose to do right now."

It didn't sound like a desperate plea to win her back.

It sounded like a threat.

As if she'd be scared of some washed-up British bachelor who'd fallen so far, he was hiding out in the middle of nowhere teaching French to future farmers of America. Even if he was the one playing with spray paint in the middle of the night, or jerking off courtesy of his digital camera, it was a coward's revenge, and cowards didn't scare her.

"Bye, bye, Jack," she chirped, and headed for the door.

"This is a mistake, Kaia." His low, angry voice followed her out. "You're going to wish you hadn't done that."

Doubtful.

Harper had been looking forward to a nice, quiet evening at home in front of the TV, hoping to lose herself in some cheesy MTV reality show—other people's misery was so much more fun than her own. But it wasn't to be. . . .

"Mind if I join you, hon?" Her mother didn't wait for an answer before squeezing next to Harper on the threadbare couch. Parents could be so inconvenient sometimes.

Harper nodded and tried to hold back a sigh. "Whatever." She upped the volume on the TV in anticipation of her mother's inevitable commentary.

"Is that the girl from that show on HBO?" her mother asked, peering at the screen. "Oh, wait, no, she has blond hair. But is she—"

"Mom! She's a real person, okay?" Harper explained, more harshly than she'd intended. "It's a *reality* show. They're all real. No actors. Get it?"

"No need to yell, dear, I'm sitting right here," Amanda Grace said dryly, raising her eyebrows. For a few minutes they watched together in blessed silence, then, "Wait, I thought she was dating that other boy? The one with the Mohawk?"

"She *was,* Mother."

"But then what's she doing with this one? And are they really going to—oh! Can they show that on TV? What are you watching?"

"It's just a show, Mom." Harper slouched down on the couch, wishing she'd chosen a different channel. Was there anything more embarrassing than watching on-screen sex with your *mother*?

"Harper, I hope that if you . . . well, if there's anything you want to talk about, you know, in that department—"

Correction: Talking about your own sex life—or, at the moment, lack thereof—with your mother was definitely more embarrassing.

"Mom, there's nothing to discuss. Trust me."

"I do, honey, it's just—" Fortunately, the scene shifted, and her mother gasped. "Is that vodka? And those two girls, what are they—? Is this really what you teenagers are doing with yourselves these days?"

"It's TV, Mom," Harper pointed out, feeling simultaneous twinges of pride and guilt that she'd been able to keep her mother so successfully in the dark.

"*Reality* TV."

Harper shook her head. "There's nothing real about any of this crap," she argued. "It's all edited to make it more exciting, and you know they're just acting up for the camera. No one's like that in real life."

Harper flipped the channel over to one of those 'All Women, All the Time' stations, hoping her mother would get absorbed by some soapy sob story and forget all about her. It wouldn't be the first time.

"I haven't seen Adam around here lately," her mother suddenly said, still staring at the TV. "Or Miranda."

Maybe she wasn't so oblivious after all.

"They're around," Harper said softly. She wasn't about to unload on her mother—last time she'd actually confided in one of her parents, she'd been barely out of diapers—but the temptation was there. There was something to be said for unconditional parental adoration, especially when everyone else you care about has decided you're worthless and unlovable.

"What's going on with you these days?" her mother asked, finally turning to her and smoothing down Harper's unruly hair, just like she used to do when Harper was younger. "You seem . . . sad."

Harper shrugged. "You know teenagers, Mom. We're a moody bunch."

"I know *you*," her mother countered. "I know when something's wrong. It might help to talk about it."

"No it won't." She knew she sounded sullen and sulky, like a little kid, but she couldn't help herself.

"Honey, I know high school can be tough—I wasn't born middle-aged, you know. But you've got to remember, it's not everything. The things that seem so horrible now, they'll pass. You'll get through it. Everyone does."

"Can we just not talk about this? Please?" *This* was why Harper never told her parents anything. They didn't get it. Harper knew her mother would probably think she just had some kind of teenybopper crush on Adam, that she and Miranda were just having a little spat that could be solved with ice cream and a smile. Having been a teenager once, a million years ago, didn't qualify her mother to understand what she was going through—and it obviously didn't give her any idea what Harper's life was like, how hard it could be.

"Of course," her mother said, lifting the remote and flipping through the channels until she stumbled upon a showing of *The Princess Bride*. "How about we just watch the movie?"

Loving this movie was one of the few things they still had in common. They'd watched it together about twenty times, and had memorized almost every line. Harper's mother switched off the light and draped a heavy blanket over both of them. Harper smiled, letting herself get carried away by the familiar jokes and the sappy but irresistible love story. If only life were as clear-cut as it was in the movies—if only you could slay a few Rodents of Unusual Size, battle your way across the Fire Swamp, slay an evil count, and get what you most desired. It would be an improvement over the real world, where danger snuck up on you and courage was so much more difficult to find.

"Harper?"

"Mmm?"

"You know your father and I love you, right?"

Of course she knew it. But it never hurt to hear it again. She focused intently on the screen and blinked back tears as Princess Buttercup threw herself into the arms of her one true love.

"Yeah," she murmured softly, leaning her head against her mother's shoulder. "You too."

# chapter

## 7

The administration had worked overtime to get everything ready for the governor's visit. The press—or, at least, a photographer from the *Grace Herald* and a reporter from the *Ludlow Times*—was due first thing that morning to take pictures of the school, which had been sufficiently buffed and shined for the occasion. A selection of high-achieving students had been carefully selected to speak with the reporter, and the crown jewel of Principal Lowenstein's presentation to the media was about to be unveiled.

Hanging over the front doors of the school, hidden by a white drop cloth, was the principal's pet project: a giant billboard, labored over by the art teacher and his most talented students. It would soon welcome the governor to town—but now, in an almost as important moment, it would serve as the face Haven High would show to the world.

Principal Lowenstein allowed herself a moment to dream—thanks to the governor's star power, the local story would be picked up by the state press, perhaps even nationally syndicated. The paparazzi were everywhere, and you never knew what might excite the tabloids. She suppressed a smile, imagining her face staring back at her from the supermarket checkout aisle. She would be seen all over the country for what she truly was: a capable, zealous administrator destined for greater things.

Specifically, destined to get the hell out of this dinky town and take on a *real* school, a place where the students cared about more than football scores and truck engines, and the teachers actually understood the material they were supposed to teach.

Proud grin firmly planted on her face, Lowenstein waved to the reporters, posed for their flashes, and pulled down the drop cloth.

And because she was so intent on staring into the camera, she was the last to see it.

The art department had gone above and beyond, pulling a campaign photo of the governor riding a horse, and blowing it up so he appeared to be galloping toward the doors of Haven High. In large type, the caption beneath the image read—or was supposed to read—HAVEN HIGH WELCOMES OUR GOVERNOR—THE BEST IN THE WEST!

It was a masterpiece of administrative banality—or would have been, had someone not snuck beneath the drop cloth, pulled out their spray paint, and made a few . . . minor changes.

The governor was now truly *riding* the horse—as one imagined he might ride his wife. The new caption: HAVEN HIGH WELCOMES OUR GOVERNOR—THE BEST LOVER IN THE WEST!

It was juvenile, lame, inappropriate, grotesque and, all in all, a reasonably accurate representation of everything Haven High stood for.

The reporter scribbled madly, and Principal Lowenstein smiled uselessly for the camera, no longer looking forward to her front-page coverage. *Welcome to Haven High,* she thought dejectedly, *where dreams come to die.*

Everyone in school that day was consumed with the question of who had pulled the prank. Everyone except Beth, who had only one thought in her mind: Who would the winner be?

That morning in homeroom, she, Harper, and the other contenders had traipsed down to the principal's office and read their speeches into the PA system. Beth assumed no one was listening—the morning's gossip was too fresh for anyone to take a break and actually pay attention—but she still felt a tiny thrill having her voice piped throughout the school, knowing that soon people would be voting on whether or not they'd been suitably impressed.

Beth wasn't thrilled with her speech, but even in her nervousness she could tell it was better than anything anyone else had to offer. Harper's, especially—from the grammatical errors to the logical inconsistencies, to the blithe suggestion that school be made several hours shorter and students be allowed to choose their own subjects of study—Beth was sure she couldn't lose.

Still, she didn't like waiting.

The announcement came in last period, toward the end of French class. Normally, Beth detested sitting through those forty-seven minutes, feeling Jack Powell's eyes upon her—it forced her to remember the day he'd kissed her in the deserted newsroom, a moment she'd been struggling for months to forget. She could, if she allowed herself, still feel his hands gripping her body, and the flicker of fear that she wouldn't be able to push him away. It made her feel dirty, and somehow trapped, as if a part of her were still stuck there with him, in that cramped, dark room.

But today, she'd been too distracted by worries about the speech to pay much attention to Powell, and that, at least, was a blessing.

"Attention, students." As the PA speaker crackled to life, Beth looked up from her desk. This was it, she knew it. Just as she knew without looking that, three rows back, Harper was watching her.

She looked, anyway.

"Students, I'm pleased to announce the results of our speech contest," the principal announced, sounding distinctly happier than she had that morning. "All the submissions were quite impressive, but after tallying the votes, we have a clear-cut winner."

Beth held her breath. Harper continued to stare.

"The student selected should report to me after school, in order to discuss the arrangements for the speech."

Beth tucked a strand of hair behind her ear and tried to look calm, as if none of this mattered.

"And the student selected for this great honor is . . . Harper Grace." Beth felt all the breath leak out of her in a loud sigh. She felt like a flat tire, empty and ready to crumple. Behind her, she knew, Harper was still watching. Only now, she'd be smiling.

"I hope you'll all join me in congratulating Ms. Grace on her accomplishment. I know she will represent the school with honor and—if you'll pardon the pun—grace."

No one laughed. And no one applauded, or whistled, or did anything to make it appear they thought this was a big deal. Which, Beth supposed, it wasn't—except to her.

If she'd only turned in the other speech, the *good* speech, this wouldn't have happened. If she hadn't cared so much about following the rules, she wouldn't have lost. She was sure of it.

Harper, after all, never followed the rules—and she always won.

Harper caught up with her after class. "Why so glum?" she asked brightly. Beth tried to walk faster, but Harper picked up speed as well, refusing to fall behind. "Oh, don't be a sore loser," Harper chided, her voice saccharine sweet. "Your speech was good . . . or at least better than mine."

"I know," Beth said quietly, bitterly. When would Harper finally leave her alone?

"But it didn't matter, of course." Harper shook her head sorrowfully.

"And why's that?" Beth half expected her to admit she'd rigged the contest. After all, why leave things to chance? Only losers like Beth would be that stupid, right?

"It wouldn't matter if you'd written the Gettysburg address," Harper explained—and Beth would think her voice almost kind, if she didn't know better, if she hadn't seen the look in Harper's eye. "You think anyone actually cared what those speeches said? You think anyone but you was listening? It was a popularity contest. Everything in high school is a popularity contest." *And how could you get this far before figuring that out?* her look said. *I thought you were supposed to be the smart one.* "That's why I'll always win. People love me. You can't beat that."

"Not everyone loves you," Beth pointed out, amazed that, for once, she wasn't frozen and brought to tears by her anger. "Not Adam."

Harper didn't even flinch. She just smiled indulgently, as if watching a child try fruitlessly to contact the outside world on a plastic telephone.

Certain she could crack the facade, Beth pushed ahead. "None of these people have figured out who you really are. But Adam gets it—now."

"What do you know about it?" Harper asked in a perfectly measured voice.

"I know that whatever you try to take from me, you'll never get what you really want," Beth snapped. "He won't stop following me around—but he's done with you, forever."

"Nothing's forever."

"Nothing's more pathetic than watching someone chase after a guy who obviously wants nothing to do with her."

Harper shook her head. "Better watch out—this bitch thing doesn't suit you. And it can't possibly have a happy ending."

"What's that supposed to mean?"

"Just a piece of friendly advice," Harper said, offering a cool smile, "from one bitch to another."

She walked away, leaving Beth alone in the middle of

the hallway, surrounded by the surging crowd of students all with better places to be. She'd finally found the nerve to stand up for herself—and Harper had barely noticed. Maybe she didn't really care about Adam, Beth realized, or about anyone but herself. Maybe that's the kind of person you had to be to wreck other people's lives.

Yet again, Harper had stolen something from her—and obviously she'd only done it to make Beth more miserable than ever. It made her even more desperate to strike back. But how could you hurt someone who didn't have the capacity to feel pain?

*She's wrong,* Harper repeated silently, over and over again.

Beth didn't know anything about Harper, and she didn't know Adam as well as she'd thought, and that should be enough to make her words powerless. *Words can never hurt me,* she sang to herself, as if this were a Very Special Episode of *Sesame Street*: "B is for Bitch."

Beth was just lashing out, feebly trying to make herself feel better—and it was only an accident that she'd struck a nerve. But Harper couldn't help wondering whether that mattered. A stopped clock is right twice a day; maybe every once in a while Beth's bitter, nonsensical babbling stumbled into the truth.

She considered ditching her meeting with the principal and escaping in search of some way to clear her mind. And maybe she would have, if she'd had Miranda by her side, ready to ply her with cigarettes and chocolate chip cookies and assure her, with the certainty of someone who knew from personal experience, that soon enough, Adam would fall prey to her natural charm.

But since she was on her own, as usual, she strode down to the principal's office, her step steady and with a hint of a bounce so that no one watching would guess the truth. And the truth was that Beth's words still echoed in her mind:

*He's done with you.*

*Forever.*

And every time she thought of them, it felt like her bones were snapping and her muscles dissolving, so that it soon took all her effort not to crumple to the floor.

"Congratulations, Ms. Grace!" the principal boomed, meeting her in the doorway with a hearty handshake. "How does it feel?"

Harper returned the smile, tossed her hair over her shoulder, and looked the principal straight in the eye. "It feels great," she said, wishing they offered an Oscar for Best Performance in a High School Hallway. "I couldn't be happier."

Suspension wasn't all bad.

In fact, as it turned out, it wasn't bad at all.

Adam slept late, ordered pizza, watched TV and, in other words, did whatever the hell he wanted to do. It's not like his mother was home enough to care. She hadn't even noticed he wasn't going to school. (And, since he'd successfully forged her signature on the suspension form, there was no reason to think that she ever would.) It wasn't a bad life. And the coach was right: It gave him plenty of time to think.

That's what he did all morning, whether he was gnawing cold pizza or flipping aimlessly between ESPN and *The*

*Backyardigans.* He thought about what had been done to him, and how he'd been wronged, and he thought about how there seemed to be no way out. And when the thoughts built up inside his head and it felt like the pressure would cause his eyes to bulge out, that's when he finally threw on some clothes and a pair of old sneakers and shambled down the street to a dark bar where they wouldn't bother to check his ID or ask why an eighteen-year-old local basketball star would want to waste his afternoon slouched over a mug of cheap, stale Bud Light.

*Like father, like son,* a voice in his head chanted.

After only a few days, he'd settled into a comfortable routine—and would be almost sorry when the suspension was lifted. Traipsing from class to class—facing his teachers, his ex-friends, his failures—was no match for long, lazy afternoons that turned into long evenings, hidden away in the dark, cozy recesses of the Lost and Found.

Sometimes he struck up a conversation with a regular—they were all regulars, here—and sometimes he kept to himself, his glowering expression keeping the prying strangers away.

"Hey, honey."

Today, apparently, wasn't going to be one of those days.

"What's a nice kid like you doing in a dump like this?"

Adam looked up from his beer. The pickup line was almost older than she was, though not by much. The woman who'd scraped her bar stool over toward him and was now curling a stubby finger through a lock of her platinum blond hair was probably a couple of years younger than his mother. She wore a garish flowered blouse whose neckline plunged far lower than you might have wanted it to, and her nails were painted a bright pink that clashed with her red pants. Each had a little decal painted on its tip. On the nail of her index finger—which she was using to trace the rim of his half-empty glass—there was a tiny butterfly.

"How about it, hon, you got a story you want to tell?"

"Not really," Adam mumbled. But he gave her a half smile. She'd been pretty, once—and at the moment, he had nothing better to do. "How about you?"

"Oh, sweetie!" She threw back her head and laughed, and he could see the blackened enamel fillings lining her molars. "I got about a million of them. Let me tell you—"

"Here I am, Adam."

He froze as a pair of arms wrapped around him from behind, cool hands pressing his chest. Which might have been a good thing, were they not hands he knew.

"Have you been waiting long?" a too-familiar voice asked.

The older woman's face reddened—though it was hard to tell, thanks to the several layers of pale pancake and blood red rouge. "I—I didn't know you had company. I, uh, I'll get out of your hair."

"She's not with me," Adam protested weakly as the hands traced their way up his body and began doing something unspeakably pleasurable to the tips of his ears. And the woman disappeared into the shadowy recesses of the bar—there were plenty of other men drinking alone.

"What do you want?" Adam asked Kaia dully, without turning around or pushing her away. He hated her . . . but he had never been able to push her away. "I was busy, in case you didn't notice."

"I noticed," Kaia said. She let go of him—Adam tried to feel relief, but couldn't—and pulled up a stool next to his. "So, aren't you going to thank me?"

"For what?" Now that she wasn't touching him anymore, Adam's feelings were uncomplicated. He just wanted her to go away.

"For rescuing you from"—Kaia looked off in the direction the older woman had disappeared—"that."

"I can take care of myself, thanks."

"Could've fooled me."

"Kaia, if you've got something to say, just say it. I don't have time for your games."

"Fine. You want the short but sweet version? You're screwing up."

Yeah, thanks for the news flash.

"Beating people up? Getting suspended? Walking around half-drunk all the time? It's pathetic—you've got to get it together."

"What do you care?" he growled, trying to push away her words before they could do any damage. Kaia never said anything without an ulterior motive.

She also never said anything that didn't sound at least partly true. It's why she was so deadly effective.

She shrugged.

"Good point. I don't care. I'm just telling you what I see. You want to ruin your life, that's your business. I'm just bringing it to your attention. Always good to make an informed decision." She flagged down the bartender and ordered a seltzer with lime. Adam suddenly wondered what she was doing here, in this dead-end bar in the middle of the afternoon, but forced himself not to ask. With Kaia, curiosity was just another form of weakness.

"I'm ruining my life?" he said instead, pouring on the sarcasm. "That's a good one. And I suppose you're just here for the show? You had nothing to do with it?"

"Very mature, Adam, blaming me for all your problems." She remained infuriatingly serene. Suddenly, she seemed to spot someone in the back of the bar, and she abruptly lifted her drink and stood up. "I've got better things to do than babysit you, Adam. Enjoy your beer."

"Like I really need someone like *you* looking out for me," he spit out.

Kaia looked up and down the long, empty bar, then fixed Adam with a pitying stare.

"It looks to me like I'm all you've got."

*You can't go home again.*

That was the line that swam into Beth's mind as she crouched behind a car in the parking lot, furious at herself for hiding like a coward, unable to find the strength to stand and show herself. She'd left school in search of Claire, or Abbie, or anyone from older, easier days, needing the reassurance of familiar faces, people to whom she mattered.

She'd found them, all right. And that, it seemed, had been the biggest mistake of all.

"Can you believe her?" Claire asked. She was lounging against the side of her silver Oldsmobile, while Abbie and Leslie perched on the hood of a boxy green Volvo. They were taking advantage of the picture-perfect weather, stretching out in the sun, and Beth would have joined them—until she heard the words that made her duck behind a parked car instead. "That speech was so pathetic. It was so *her,* though—all the little Miss Perfect crap."

"Come on, Claire, don't be such a bitch," Abbie said, in a chastising tone spoiled by the fact that she couldn't choke back her laughter.

"What? Admit it: She thinks she's better than everyone."

"Well . . ." Abbie and Leslie exchanged a glance. "Yeah," Leslie allowed. "But that doesn't mean—"

"Guys. Did you not see the way she was looking at us at the sleepover?"

"Like she couldn't wait to get away from us," Abbie mused.

"Like she was bored out of her mind," Leslie added. "And we were supposed to be honored or something that she'd showed up in the first place."

"It was kind of worth it, though, wasn't it?" Abbie asked, tipping her head back to get a full blast of sunshine. "I told you we'd get some good gossip out of her."

"Okay, but is it really worth putting up with Miss Priss for much longer, gossip or not?" Claire pointed out. "All this fake smiling's starting to hurt my face."

"Give her a break, Claire. This is Beth we're talking about—I mean, yeah, she's kind of boring and pretentious, but she was your best friend," Abbie reminded her.

Claire scowled. "*Was.* Note the tense. She's the one who ditched us—and now we're supposed to be grateful that she's come sniffing around again? Like we're some kind of last-resort rescue from total loserdom?"

"Okay, she's not *that* bad," Abbie argued. "It's not like we weren't friends with her . . . once."

"She's different now," Claire said firmly. "You know she's not one of us anymore. And I don't care how many innocent little wide-eyed smiles she gives us—she knows it too."

Maybe she had to work on her delivery. Giving someone helpful advice probably wasn't supposed to make them want to throw barware at you—but Adam had looked about ready to do just that. And the irony was, she'd actually been sincere. For whatever reason, she was tired of watching his pitiful downward spiral; but, apparently, he didn't want her help.

It was a good thing Kaia had better things to think about than the aberrant wave of consideration for her one-time mark. Reed was waiting.

"I'm glad you came," she said, when she found him slouched in a booth at the back of the bar. He was wearing a tight black T-shirt and, with his river of black curly hair and deep brown eyes, he almost faded into the shadows. She hadn't seen him—not this close, at least—since the day he'd run off from her house.

Her run-in with Powell had convinced her once and for all that if anyone in her life was a desperate perv, it was him. Reed had no motivation to torment her since she was sure he didn't know about Powell. She'd been too careful.

"I'm not doing this, Kaia." She loved the way it sounded when he said her name in his lazy, throaty voice. It sounded like honey—with a splash of tequila thrown in for flavoring.

"Doing what?" Kaia was good at acting the innocent, but in this case, she was honestly clueless. And she didn't like it.

"You and your father—I'm not getting in the middle of that."

"Of what? There is no 'that.' He barely knows I exist. And I try my best to forget he does."

"I saw what you were doing."

He spoke so slowly, as if each word did battle to escape from his brain. Usually it was sexy. Now it was just maddening. "Using me, to piss him off. I'm not doing it."

Kaia laughed. Unlike the light tinkling giggle she usually allowed herself, this was a full-throated chuckle, a mix of relief and genuine amusement. She stopped abruptly when she noticed his expression—apparently, Reed didn't like it when people laughed at him.

"Reed, did you see the look on my father's face when he went back into the house? Did you hear what he said? He doesn't care what I do. If I wanted to piss him off, I'd spill something on his white Alsatian carpeting. He couldn't care less about my dating life."

"I know what I heard," Reed persisted.

His stubbornness, usually so sexy, was going to ruin everything.

"You've seen too many movies. My father and I? It's not like that. What you heard was the same fight my father and I have every time we speak—which is about once a month. I don't care what he thinks of me, or who I'm with." She didn't say *please believe me.* Either he would or he wouldn't. "My father has nothing to do with—with whatever is happening between us," she swore. "Forget him. I have."

Reed considered her for a moment. He pushed a hand through his unruly hair, then nodded. "Okay."

"We're good?" she asked, wrapping her hands around his.

He nodded again. "We're good."

She leaned across the table to kiss him, hovering there for as long as she could, tasting his lips and breathing in his deep, musky scent. Then she stood up and laid her cell phone and wallet down on the table, hoping she'd chosen a clean spot.

"In that case, I'm off to find what passes for a bathroom in this place." She skimmed her fingers across his forehead—for no reason other than that she liked to touch him. "Don't go away."

Kaia had been gone for two minutes when her cell phone beeped. Reed could still smell her perfume lingering in the air.

The phone beeped again. A second text message. And Kaia was nowhere in sight.

The phone was lying on the table, only a few inches away. It beeped a third time, insistent, as if it were calling to him.

Reed wasn't usually a curious person. He saw as much of the world as the world wanted him to see—no more, no less. Why examine something when you could just breathe it in and enjoy?

But Kaia was different.

She was complicated and surprising. He didn't trust himself around her. And he didn't trust her at all.

When the phone beeped a fourth time, he looked quickly back toward the bathroom. There was no sign of her, so he picked up the phone and flipped it open.

See you at 8.
Wear the black teddy I like.
Or nothing.
That's even better. J

Reed had never been a big reader. And in English class—when he bothered to attend—he'd always ignored all the crap about levels and symbolism. But the message didn't require much interpretation; it said exactly what it meant.

When Kaia got through with him this afternoon, she'd be meeting someone else.

And maybe Reed was better at interpretation than he'd thought, because he was suddenly convinced that this was someone Kaia had seen a lot. "J" had certainly seen plenty—*all*—of her.

Reed wasn't usually a possessive person. A hookup wasn't a marriage proposal. People didn't belong to each other. He belonged only to himself—and his girls were the same.

But Kaia was different.

Or at least he'd thought she was.

Reed held the phone and brought his thumb toward the delete button—and then he stopped. The phone didn't belong to him. And neither did Kaia.

He closed the phone, laying it back on the table next to her wallet.

And when Kaia came back from the bathroom, he was gone.

Beth didn't have the nerve to confront them in person. It was easier, safer to pick up the phone and climb into bed, swaddling herself in the fuzzy pink comforter. But, even surrounded by all the things she loved—Snuffy the stuffed turtle, her copy of *The Wind in the Willows,* her trophy from the sixth-grade spelling bee—she felt lost in hostile territory.

Claire picked up the phone after the fourth ring, just as Beth had begun to breathe an ounce easier and prepared herself to leave a message. "Claire, we need to talk," she began, knowing that even if the other girl still didn't have caller ID, she would recognize Beth's voice. "Are you . . . mad at me?" It sounded so childish—but it was all she could come up with. She couldn't reference what she'd heard in the parking lot.

"Why would I be mad at you, Bethie?" Claire asked, adopting the nickname she'd used when they were kids. "Have you *done* something? Feeling guilty?"

"You just seem . . . mad," Beth said lamely, avoiding the question. Did she feel guilty? Had she trashed the friendship, or had they just drifted apart? What did it say that she could no longer remember?

"Beth, I'm kind of busy. Is there a point to this? Because otherwise—"

"I heard you in the parking lot," Beth blurted. If Claire hung up, Beth might not have the nerve to call back. And that would mean letting it go, returning their fake smiles and pretending she didn't know what lay behind them. "You, Abbie, Leslie—I heard what you said. About me."

"Oh."

There was a pause. Then— "You were spying on us?"

"No, I was just—it doesn't matter. I just . . ."

"What do you want me to say?" Claire asked irritably.

"If you heard us, why are you even calling? What do you want from me?"

It was a reasonable question, but for all her agonizing over this call, Beth hadn't thought to come up with an answer.

"I wanted—I thought we could be friends again."

Claire laughed. "Just like that? Just because you decide, after all this time, you want to pick things up where we left off. You think it's that easy?"

"Why not?" Beth whispered.

"Because where were you, *Bethie*? Where were you when Abbie broke her leg, or got her first boyfriend? Where were you when I almost failed precalc? When my parents got divorced—" Her voice, which had been rising steadily, suddenly broke off, and all Beth could hear were her labored breaths.

"I'm sorry," Beth began. "I wish I hadn't—"

"I don't care if you're sorry. Don't you get that? And I don't care anymore that you weren't there—I got by without you. We all did. I don't need you anymore. And I really don't care if you need me."

Claire hung up.

Beth sat with the phone to her ear for a long time, just listening to the dial tone. That was it, then. Unless she wanted to back down and forgive Adam, she was on her own.

On her nightstand, sandwiched between a stack of CDs and an empty picture frame (that had, until recently, held a shot from the junior prom), sat a small cardboard box. It was the size of a jewelry box, and inside it lay two yellow pills, each the size of one of her gold stud earrings.

She lifted the top and looked at the pills, examining them more closely than she had before. She even took one out of the box, just to see how it would feel in the palm of her hand. It was light, like aspirin, and it looked just as harmless.

Kane had given them to her as a Christmas present. He'd thought they could make their New Year's "*ex*-tra special"—a mistake almost as big as the one she'd made by inviting him into her life in the first place.

Still, she'd pocketed the pills, and kept them. For a rainy day? If so, this qualified, and she could certainly do with a jolt of happiness, chemical or not.

But she put the pill back in the box. She either had too much restraint or not enough nerve—she was no longer sure which. She didn't want to find out what those little pills did, no matter how wrecked she felt.

Yet, for whatever reason, she couldn't bring herself to throw them away.

# chapter

## 8

A month of detention was starting to look a whole lot sweeter. Room 246 was the same as she remembered it from her last week of incarceration: a long, gray space crammed with rows of desks drilled to the floor, the detention monitor positioned at the front with her nose buried in a book. There were just a few key differences.

First, Harper wasn't by her side to help make the hours speed by.

Second, the sign-in sheet was now yellow, rather than its former puke green.

And third, the only difference that mattered: Kane Geary was sitting in the back corner. And he was flagging her down, pointing to the empty desk to his left.

*Me?* Miranda mouthed, fighting the urge to look behind her and see what tall, leggy blonde was the true target of that lazy grin.

*Yes, you.* He nodded, and when she slipped into the desk beside him, he patted her on the knee in welcome. It was all Miranda could do to not slide off the seat and melt onto the floor.

"Welcome to prison," he greeted her. "At least now I've got a good cell mate."

The hour passed too quickly, in a haze of whispered complaints about the monitor's hairy mole or the leaning Mohawk of the delinquent in front of them. They played dirty hangman (Miranda's winning word: "vulva"), placed bets on the number of wads of gum stuck beneath Kane's desk (seven), and, for a blissful ten minutes, Kane leaned over to Miranda's notebook and drew nasty but spot-on caricatures of the other members of the basketball team, who were seated in a hulking cluster toward the front of the room. Blissful because, to reach Miranda's notebook, Kane had to shift his body into her space and lay his arm across her desk, where it pressed, very lightly, against her own. As he stared at the page, intent on getting the point guard's dopey expression just right, Miranda concentrated on his arm, imagining that he was touching her on purpose. Knowing, even when he shifted position for a moment and his hand actually grazed hers, that he wasn't.

And then the bell rang, and it was all over.

It would be asking too much, holding out foolish hope to think that—

"See you tomorrow?" Kane asked, hoisting his bag over his shoulder and helping her gather up her scattered belongings.

"Same time, same place," Miranda replied, trying desperately for nonchalance.

Thank God Beth had weaseled out of trouble and left Miranda to face her punishment all on her own.

Miranda Stevens had spent her whole life flying under the radar and doing what other people told her to do.

So this is what you got for being a rebel?

Bring it on.

Beth felt him before she heard him. She was absorbed in her work, proofing the page layout for the next issue of the paper, and didn't hear the door to the tiny office click open. But some part of her must have registered it, and must have known whose hand lay on the knob, because gradually the words on her computer screen began to swim in front of her eyes and, unable to concentrate, she sensed a heavy quality in the air. The walls felt closer, the ceiling lower, and her muscles tensed.

He cleared his throat.

It was then she knew for sure.

"I thought we had an agreement," Beth said, trying to keep the quaver out of her voice. Her hands gripped the edge of the small computer desk until her knuckles turned white. She focused on the dull pain of the wooden desk digging into her palms. It kept her from being swept off in a wave of panicked thoughts—the room was empty, the halls were deserted, he was blocking the only exit, there would be no one to hear her scream. Yes, it was probably best to steer clear of thoughts like that, and not to even think the word "scream." Or she just might.

"You're not supposed to be in here, not while I'm here alone." It was silly, but she suddenly felt she'd made a dangerous misstep by calling attention to the fact that she was by herself—as if, otherwise, he wouldn't have noticed.

"Things have changed," Jack Powell said. He locked the

door behind him and took a seat on the couch, patting the space next to him. Then he laughed at the look of horror on her face. "Oh, calm down," he said irritably. "You've got nothing I want."

Beth couldn't believe she'd once found this man adorable, fantasizing about his dark eyes and crooked smile. She had, more than once, drifted off to sleep while imagining them together in a romantic scene from a black-and-white movie. Everything about him repelled her now— even the accent seemed phony.

"Get out," she said steadily. "I told you before, I'll tell the administration what happened, what—you tried to do, if you don't leave me alone."

The last time they'd talked one-on-one and she'd unveiled this threat, it had knocked him off balance. But this time was different. He was expecting it—and more than that, he seemed to welcome it.

"Get off it, Beth. I didn't *do* anything to you. We both know that you wanted—" He cut himself off and gave himself a little shake. "Enough of that." And suddenly, his cold look was replaced by an amicable grin, the same one that made every other girl in school swoon. The sharp change, as if he'd swapped personalities with the flip of a switch, was the scariest thing of all. "That's why I stopped by," he said pleasantly, as if she'd invited him in for tea. "To tell you that the past is behind us. You won't be going to the administration, or making any more threats, and I'll do whatever it is I want to do."

"And how do you figure that?" Beth asked, forcing herself not to look away. Facing this Powell was even more unsettling than confronting him in attack mode. At least then, she knew what to prepare herself for. Now, looking at his blank face, she could only image what lay beneath the surface. This was the face she still saw in her nightmares.

"You made a good show of it, Beth, and I'll agree, you had something on me. Impressive. But, unfortunately, I now have something on you." He pulled a folded-up page out of his pocket. Beth knew what it was before he'd unfolded it and waved it in the air like a conqueror's flag. The blood red color gave it away. "I've got proof," Powell said simply.

"What you did is worse," she whispered—any louder, and she couldn't trust her voice not to break.

"Maybe," he allowed. "But you've no evidence of that. My word against yours, remember? And as for this"—he waved the flyer again—"I'm afraid I've got all the evidence I need. Ask your little friend Miranda if you don't believe me. I presume you'll find her in detention." He shook his head. "Nice of you to stand up and face the music with her, by the way. That was a classy move."

Beth felt a blast of shame rise to her cheeks. "So we're even," she said, fighting against the suspicion that it wouldn't be quite that easy. "I've got something on you, and you've got something on me."

"Not quite," he stopped her. "As I see it, since I'm the only one here with any kind of proof, you've got nothing on me. Any accusation you make now is tainted. Nothing more than a pathetic attempt to get yourself out of trouble by discrediting me. No more than you'd expect from a coward who lets her partner take the blame."

She sighed. "What do you want?"

"Nothing. For now." Powell leaned back on the couch and kicked his feet up. "I just wanted to alert you that there was a new game afoot. Oh, don't look so glum," he admonished, twisting his face into a parody of her own miserable scowl. "This means we can be friends again, just like in the old days—back when you were *so* eager to help me out."

Beth remembered. It made her want to throw up.

"And if you're nice, there are things I can do for you too," Powell said.

"Like what?" she asked snidely.

"Like, for example, telling you who turned you in. Like they say, the best cure for losing one battle is winning the next. I'm sure you'd like to get even with *someone,* and since it's not going to be me . . ."

She knew it would be stupid to play any more of his games, but could it hurt to stay a moment longer, to smile and ask nicely? To get a name?

She was tired of being a victim. Maybe Powell was right: Just because she'd lost this battle didn't mean it was time to give up.

Maybe it was just time to find a better target.

And reload.

She felt like a Bond girl, or a savvy spy from *Mission: Impossible,* as she snaked her way through the crowd and took position, waiting patiently to deploy her grand master plan.

*We need to talk,* her note had said. *Meet me on the 6 P.M. Twilight Trails train. I'll be in the front seat of the second car from the back. Beth*

The Twilight Trails company ran fake freight trains on a scenic route through the desert every day at sunset. They stopped at Grace, then continued on for an hour into the wilderness before turning around. Which meant that she and Adam would be trapped together for two hours. And unless he wanted to throw himself from a moving—albeit painfully slow-moving—train, he would be forced to listen to what she had to say.

She paid her exorbitant fee and settled into a window seat, glancing disdainfully at the scattering of passengers around her, wondering who would actually waste their money on a tour of this wasteland. She put on a pair of sunglasses—all the better to play out her interlude in espionage—and pulled out a magazine.

She didn't have to wait long.

"I was so glad to get your note—" Adam began, his voice breaking off when she turned her face from the window. "What the hell are you doing here?"

Harper tried to smile and ignore his tone—and his disappointment. "I guess the jig is up," she quipped.

"What is this?" Adam asked, whirling around to scan the rest of the train car. "Where's Beth?"

He could be so slow sometimes . . . but, still, so adorable.

"Beth's not coming," Harper said, spelling out the obvious. "I sent the note."

He shook his head. "You're really sick, you know that?" He turned on his heel and walked back down the aisle, taking a seat toward the back of the train car.

Harper sighed, stood up, and followed him, ignoring the glare of the conductor, who cleared his throat and pointed at the large red letters ordering passengers to STAY SEATED WHILE THE TRAIN IS IN MOTION.

"It's not that big a car," she pointed out, sitting down behind Adam. If she squeezed in next to him, it might scare him away. "Do we really need to play musical chairs?" She sat on her knees and leaned forward, resting her arms on the seat in front of her. He didn't turn his face up to look at her, but if he had, her lips would still have been too far away to brush his forehead. "Train doesn't stop again until Salina," she pointed out. "You're stuck with me."

Adam closed his eyes and began to rub the bridge of his nose. "Fine. What do you want from me?"

"I want to know what you want from *me*, Ad. What can I do to fix things? Just tell me."

"Nothing," he grunted.

"You can't stay mad forever."

"Watch me."

They sat in silence for a moment. Harper watched the scenery crawl by, mile after mile of low ranging hills and straggly scrub brush. All painted in the monotonous sepia tones of desert life. *Who would search this out?* she wondered again. *Who would pay?* One elderly woman across the aisle wasn't even looking out the window. Instead, she had her eyes glued to a trashy romance novel, as if the scenery was beside the point.

"So," Harper began again, casually, "who do you think spray-painted the billboard? My money's on the sophomores— it was so lame. Reeks of some pathetic attempt to establish a rep. As if—"

"Don't do that," he said abruptly.

"What?"

"Don't act like everything's normal."

"It *can* be," she pointed out. Pleaded.

"No."

She'd tried being patient and giving him his space, but that just wasn't her. She couldn't just wait—she needed to *act*. She refused to let Beth win, and she was physically incapable of just letting him go. If it meant sacrificing her precious dignity and making him understand how much she needed him, then that's just what she would do. And so she'd formulated her plan, and now she just needed to push through his anger and pride, and uncover that piece of him that still loved her.

"Adam, you want Beth to forgive you, right?"

"Don't talk about her."

"I know you do. Everyone sees you running around school after her and—"

"I said, *don't* talk about her."

"Okay, fine. I just . . . I just don't get it. How can you expect . . . some people to forgive you, but you won't forgive me?"

"It's not the same," he snapped.

"But, why? Okay, I lied—so did you. I screwed up—so did you. And I still love—"

"It's. Not. The. Same," he repeated.

"You're right, because what you and I had together, it's nothing like you and Beth. It's so much more—"

"You really want to know?" he asked, loudly enough that the woman across the aisle looked up from her book in alarm. He whirled around to look at Harper, who resisted the urge to sink back into her own seat and turn her face away from his expression and what it meant.

"Of course I do."

"No, you don't."

"*Yes,* I really do." Though she wasn't sure it was true. "Tell me. Why can't we just get past this?"

"Because it's not what you did!" he yelled, as if he'd been holding the words in for weeks and they had finally battled their way out. They were all looking at her now: the old woman across the aisle, the mother with two squirming kids who kept shooting her a sympathetic smile, the preteen girls two rows ahead who couldn't even be bothered to disguise their eager eavesdropping. Harper knew exactly how pathetic she must look, but she forced herself not to care what a train full of tourists thought of her. Today only one person's opinion mattered.

*It's not what you did.* Then . . . what?

"It's who you *are,* Harper," he said, more quietly. This was how a doctor's face must look when he's telling someone the patient died, Harper realized. Adam was pronouncing their relationship. Time of death, 6:09.

"I don't get it," she said, but that was just another lie. After all, hadn't she already been treated to this little speech? Hadn't she already been informed of what a horrible, irredeemable piece of trash Harper Grace had become?

"Look, with Kane, what he did? It was shitty, but . . . no big surprise. I knew better than to trust him. But you?" Adam sighed. "I always trusted you. Out of everyone, you were the only one . . ."

"That's what I'm saying, Ad," Harper begged. "It's different between the two of us. You can't let one screwup ruin everything."

"It's not just about that," Adam said. "It doesn't matter if

I forgive you. I can't be with someone like you. Or be around someone like you. Not someone who'd do what you did."

"Someone like me?" Harper cried. "Someone who's been your best friend since you were eight years old?"

He shook his head.

"You're not that person. I thought you were, but . . . something's different. You're . . ."

"What?"

"I don't know."

"*What?* Just say it."

"Wrong. Okay? Something in you, it's like . . . it's gone bad. Rotted."

Harper just looked at him, her eyes watering, her hair falling down over her face. Surely he would look at her and see that she *was* still the same person, that however much of a bitch she could be, it didn't define her. She'd done the wrong thing, she conceded that—but it didn't mean there was nothing right left in her. It wasn't fair for him to think that. It wasn't right for him to say it.

And when he saw how he'd hurt her . . .

But he did look at her, and his face didn't soften; in fact, his mouth tightened into a hard, firm line. And then he turned away and settled back into his seat.

"I told you that you wouldn't want to hear it," he said, and his voice was casual, almost sneering, as if he couldn't hear her collapsed onto the seat behind him, choking back her sobs. But of course he heard; he just didn't care.

"Want some?"

Beth shuddered. She'd come out here hoping to be alone. No one used the playground this time of night, and she figured there'd be no one to see her huddled under a tree, her knees tucked up to her chest and her eyes filled with tears. Fleeing from Powell, she'd needed to go somewhere safe, and for Beth, the playground felt like home. All the more reason to be displeased when some stoner in a weathered leather jacket and torn black jeans slumped down beside her, waving a joint in her face. (At least, Beth assumed that's what it was—she'd never seen one in real life, not this close.)

She shook her head and laid it back down on her knees, hoping that if she closed her eyes and ignored him, maybe he would slink away.

"I just figured, you know, your eyes are going to be all red, anyway," the guy explained. "So, might as well take advantage of it."

She didn't say anything.

"Pot joke," he said. "Not funny, I guess." He paused, and she could hear him inhale deeply. "Look, you sure you don't want any? You look like you could use . . ."

Beth looked up then, and faced him with a fierce expression, silently daring him to finish the sentence. That's all she needed to hear right now, some burnout telling her that she was an uptight "Miss Priss" who could use a little fun in her life. She didn't know whether he was trying to insult her or pick her up, but either way, she wasn't in the mood.

"A break," he concluded, blowing out a puff of smoke. "Bad day, huh? Me too."

"I'm sorry, I really don't want to be rude, but I don't even know you, and—"

"Reed," he said, raising the joint as if to toast her. "Rhymes with weed."

She rolled her eyes.

"Another joke," he added. "Still not funny?"

It suddenly occurred to Beth that she was alone on a deserted playground with this guy—anything could happen. But whether it was his amiable expression or her exhaustion, she didn't feel threatened, just worn out. "Like I was saying, I came here to be alone, and I'm sure you're a nice guy and all, but—"

"I'm not trying to pick you up," he said suddenly.

"What?"

"Too much trouble." He leaned back against the tree, staring up at the sky. "Girls. Women. Whatever you call yourselves. I'm out."

"Uh, congratulations?"

"Damn right." Reed closed his eyes and took another hit.

"So what do you want, then?"

"World peace? A Fender Stratocaster?" he grinned. "How 'bout a warm breeze and a good buzz?"

"What do you want from *me*?" Beth clarified, not sure whether to be annoyed or amused. "If you're not trying to pick me up, what are you doing?"

"You were crying," he said, as if that explained everything.

"And?"

"And I wanted to make you stop. Which you did."

"Oh." Beth blushed, feeling a little silly for having assumed some dark ulterior motive.

"But if you want to be alone . . ."

She realized that was the last thing she wanted. "No, stay—I mean, you can. If you want."

Reed shrugged. "Whatever." Raising his eyebrows, he

tipped the joint toward her again. She waved him away. Not that tuning out didn't seem like a pretty good idea right about now, but it wouldn't solve anything. And it's not like Reed looked particularly cheerful himself.

"I'm Beth," she blurted, blushing again. He hadn't asked for her name, probably didn't even care.

Reed shifted away from the tree, lying flat on his back with his arms splayed out to his sides. A slow smile broke across his face. "Beth Manning. Yeah, I know."

"What do you think you're doing?" Kaia hissed as soon as Powell picked up the phone.

"Right now? Grading papers and trying not to vomit over the sad state of secondary education in this country."

"Don't be cute. I assume you were there." She hoped her voice wasn't betraying how much this pervy stalking routine was freaking her out. So she focused on her anger—it gave her clarity.

"*Cute* is not something I aspire to be at the moment. Enlightened might be a better goal to strive for. Care to fill me in on what's got you so hot and bothered?"

"I got your text message, Jack—and so did he, just like you intended."

"He? He who?" He sounded so genuinely clueless that Kaia was certain it was an act; nothing about Powell had ever been genuine.

"Drop it. You know I was with Reed. I know you saw me with him. You probably followed me there." Kaia could almost see it—his figure, waiting in the dark, coldly weighing his options, delighting in his view. She shivered.

"Are you actually admitting that you were with someone else?" Now his tone shifted from innocence to outrage. "And I'm supposed to feel *guilty* because my intimate message somehow fell into the wrong hands? Seems like the only guilty party here, *mon amour,* is you."

"I'm supposed to believe it was just a coincidence?" Kaia laughed bitterly. "Right. Just leave me alone, okay? This is it. We're done."

"I don't think that's your decision to make," Powell said, his voice low and steady. "Only one thing is done here, and it's your little dalliance with the Sawyer boy. I warned you before to keep your hands off."

"Or what?" Kaia struggled to keep her voice as calm as his. "You'll keep following me around until I realize you're the only man for me?"

"Oh, Kaia." Powell sighed, and took on a patronizing tone that suggested he was delivering wisdom from on high to a silly little girl. "Stalking is a coward's game. Hiding in bushes. Peering in windows." He laughed humorlessly. "Now does that really sound like me? No, when I want something, I take it."

"Not everything's yours to have," she snapped.

"Not everything, true. But you are."

"You're pathetic," she spit out.

"Now, now, that's not very nice. And as I've already suggested, you should be rather nice to me. Or do you *want* to fail your senior year? Get thrown out of school? Let's remember who's in charge here."

*Enough.*

"I am," Kaia snapped. "You know what will happen if I go to the administration and tell them how you've been forcing yourself on poor little me."

"Your word against mine," he said simply. "And once I'm through with you, your word will be worthless."

"Your word against mine and *Beth's,*" she reminded him. "Or have you forgotten I know about that little misstep?"

"Beth's been taken care of," he said shortly. "I think you'll find she won't be much interested in joining forces with your little campaign. It's over, Kaia. No more leverage. But I'm a bighearted man. If you're ready to apologize and come back to me—"

"Dream on."

"Have it your way," he said agreeably. "But I think you'll change your mind soon enough."

"Just leave me alone."

"I'm afraid I can't do that, Kaia." He chuckled again. "You know, I once suggested that you stick to playing with boys your own age. Looks like you should have taken my advice."

# chapter

## 9

"Get out."

The girl rolled over and snuggled up against him, her blond hair brushing against his lips. Kane spit it out, pushed her away.

"I said, get out." He climbed out of the bed and began gathering up her clothes, then packed them into a ball and threw them at her.

"It's so early," the girl whispered sleepily, burrowing deeper into the covers. "Come back to bed."

It was early, just past sunrise. *Time to take the trash out,* Kane thought, but chose not to say. If she wouldn't leave, he would. He couldn't stand to look at her anymore. That silky blond hair and those cornflower blue eyes had looked so appetizing the night before. Now they just looked . . . like Beth.

He slammed a fist against the wall. Damn it. Her again. He'd driven her out of his mind and now, here she was— or a pale imitation of her—in his bed.

"I'm going out," Kane growled, pulling on a T-shirt and pair of sneakers. "Be gone when I get back."

"Kane," the girl whimpered, "what did I do?"

*Let's see,* thought Kane. *You went home with some guy you met at a party, before he even knew your name. You were insipid and sloppy drunk. You were easy.*

But that wasn't really it, was it? He made two fists, digging his nails into the fleshy heel of his hand to force the thought away.

*You weren't Beth.*

He despised himself for his weakness. It was a part of himself he hated, and he'd thought he'd rooted it out years ago.

Beth was like poison to his system, corroding its works. This had to stop.

He didn't want her forgiveness.

He didn't want her back.

He wanted her gone.

*Gone. But not forgotten.*

The card was unsigned.

When the doorbell had woken her just after sunrise, Kaia had hoped it would be Reed. And when she'd opened the door to a delivery man with a long, white box of flowers, she'd hoped it would be a gift from Reed. Maybe he'd decided to call a truce and forgive her.

Hope springs eternal.

Twelve long-stemmed roses.

Each one dyed an inky black.

And that card.

*Gone. But not forgotten.*

She hadn't dropped the box in horror—she'd hurled it away from her. Roses painted the color of death flew through the room, their black petals fluttering through the air like locusts.

It would have been bad enough if she'd been absolutely sure it was Powell.

But she wasn't—and that was worse. Reed and Powell both thought she'd betrayed them; one of them was too cowardly to face her, and too obsessed to walk away.

It wasn't fear that made her hands tremble or her heart slam in her chest, she told herself. It wasn't fear that made her pace across the room, unable to sit down or stay still, made her check and double-check that she'd locked the door.

It was anger.

No one did this to Kaia Sellers.

No one had power over her like this. Kaia was the one with the power—nothing happened unless she wanted it to happen.

Hadn't she already proven that?

After all, she'd *made* him want her.

Now she could make him go away.

She could make him sorry.

*He'll be sorry. They'll all be sorry.*

Harper awoke with a gasp, the words still pounding in her ears. *They'll all be sorry.* For a moment, caught in that foggy zone between sleep and waking, the sentence had no meaning.

And then it all came flooding back.

Beth.

Miranda.

Even Adam, who had turned his back on her.

She only remembered flashes of what she'd dreamed—the screams, the silence at the end, and the feeling of satisfaction.

A cold sweat dotted her brow. As the disjointed memory of the nightmare crowded back into her mind, Harper lay still, flat on her back, staring at the cracks in the ceiling and trying not to be afraid.

She could still hear the screams.

It felt like a beast lay deep inside of her, waiting for her to relax control, so it could awake and unleash its wrath.

Harper liked to believe she was in charge. Everything she did, she did by choice.

But there were Miranda, and Adam—the two people who knew her best—and they didn't think she had a choice.

*You can't help it. You are who you are.*

They thought she couldn't help but spread her poison.

And remembering the rage that had coursed through her as she slept, Harper couldn't help but wonder: Maybe they were right.

*I was right. I knew I was right.*

Miranda stuffed the last Hershey's Kiss into her mouth and checked the clock. Six thirty A.M. She'd now officially been up all night—and had the empty bags of candy to prove it.

She'd actually gone to bed early, craving those moments before sleep when she was free to think about anything she wanted, and she could let her mind wander to Kane. In the dark she could indulge her wildest fantasies about what he might say, and how they might be together.

But her mind kept veering away from happy thoughts. It took her back toward Harper—and all her lies.

*He says he just likes you as a friend.*

*Forget him, he's an ass.*

*You'll never have him—just move on.*

*It's for your own good.*

All those months, Miranda had assumed Harper was just avoiding the obvious, ugly truth: Miranda wasn't good enough. Kane was out of her league. She'd even thought Harper was being *sweet*. Such a good friend, she'd thought, to soften the blow, obscure the truth.

As if Harper knew anything about truth.

She'd taken away the one guy Miranda had ever truly wanted and handed him to Beth. She'd excused herself with one lie after another, enjoying everything she'd ever wanted while Miranda was left feeling worthless and ugly.

But now that the lies were finished and Miranda had Kane all to herself, she was certain: It wasn't hopeless. There was something between them, even if it was only a kernel of possibility.

And what was she doing about it? Scheming and strategizing how to satisfy her deepest desires? Funneling her empty rage into a plan that would finally put Harper in her place?

Of course not.

She was eating her way through a pound of candy. She was disgusting herself.

Suddenly, Miranda felt the lump of chocolate within her transform itself into a volcano, about to erupt. She needed to purge herself of the calories and, along with them, the helplessness that must have announced to the world, *I'm nothing. Walk all over me.* She had to purify her body and herself, and then, as the sun rose, she would be ready to face the new day. Face Harper. Take care of business.

*Taking care of business.* Adam gritted his teeth at the memory. That's what Kane used to say before he went out with a girl he was planning to dump.

And then he would smile, as if it really were a business transaction. As if it were nothing.

*And here I am,* Adam thought, *dwelling and agonizing and analyzing. Like a girl.*

*So which of us is the freak?*

He'd forgotten to shut his blinds the night before, and this morning the sun had woken him. Not that he was getting much sleep these days, thanks to her.

His blood still boiled at the thought of the wasted hours sitting on that train in stony silence, pretending he couldn't hear her weep behind him.

She brought this misery on herself, he reminded himself.

She wasn't his problem anymore.

He didn't care.

He shut his blinds and, when that didn't make a satisfying enough sound, slammed his fist into the wall.

It hurt so much, he did it again.

No more, he thought. No more dwelling on Harper, letting the anger drive him through the day. And, while he was at it, no more Beth. No more mooning, following, begging, pleading. She didn't want to forgive him? Fine.

He had his dignity, and it was time Beth understood that.

Forgetting how early it was, he punched in her cell number—for the last time, he told himself. It rang and rang.

"I know you're screening," Adam said harshly after the voice mail beep. "And don't worry. I won't be bothering you anymore. If you want to be a bitch about all this, fine. I'm out."

He hung up.

He'd called her a bitch.

It felt good.

And, then, a moment later, it didn't.

"Look, I'm sorry about what I said," he began gruffly, after the beep. "You've just got to know, the way you're acting—" No, that wasn't right. He hung up again. Climbed back into bed and closed his eyes.

But he couldn't go back to sleep.

Unfinished business and all.

"I know it's crazy, calling you again, but how the hell else am I supposed to talk to you? You're so damn sure that everything—" He hung up again, almost threw the phone across the room. This was humiliating. He hated himself for doing it. Hated her for putting him through it. And yet—

"Beth. Look, I'm sorry. Please, just call me back. I—I love you. Please."

*I love you.* He'd never said the words aloud. But with Kaia, he'd thought . . . not that he did, of course—not now, not yet. But maybe someday. Or so he'd imagined.

Just goes to show he must be even stupider than people thought.

Reed pushed the pedal to the floor and the speedometer edged up to 55. The truck couldn't go any faster. It was a piece of shit, just like everything else in his life.

What had he been thinking, to imagine a girl like that would take him seriously? Her life was like a Ferrari—and his was a clunker that couldn't even hit the speed limit.

The night before, he hadn't cared. A few drinks, a few joints, and nothing mattered. But this morning, neck and back sore from sleeping on the guys' couch, it was all he could think about. He'd been stupid enough to forget who he was and ignore who she was, and he'd let himself get burned.

His guitar rattled around in the back and, suddenly, Reed made an abrupt U-turn, his tires screeching as the truck veered around and headed off down the highway, away from town and into the desert.

He would find a quiet, empty spot and play until his voice went hoarse and his fingers bled. And maybe then he would be able to purge her from his system. Or at least purge the reckless surge of anger that shot through him every time he thought of her and what might have happened.

If only he hadn't picked up her phone.

If only the truck would go faster.

If only he hadn't used up all his stash.

Things were easier when you didn't have to think.

When you didn't have to feel.

*I feel nothing*, Beth thought, watching the tiny red light flash on her phone. *I see his name flash up on the screen, again and again, and I feel . . . nothing.*

It was just after dawn and she was at work. These days she was always at work, she thought bitterly, plunging the first batch of fries into the deep fryer and switching on the coffeemaker. She couldn't complain too much; it's not like she had anywhere else to be.

The phone rang again—she stuffed it into her bag.

It was easy to hide out in the diner, losing herself in the mechanics of wiping down the counters and mopping the floors. Sometimes, she even thought she'd reached some kind of Zen state, where she could accept whatever happened and move on.

The phone rang a third time and, without warning, the wave of rage swept over her. It beat against her, pummeling her with the whys she couldn't answer. *Why me?*

That was at the top of the list.

She pictured Adam rolling around in bed with Kaia, while they were still together. She pictured Kane and his lying smile, touching her, stealing her trust. She pictured Harper whispering poisonous nothings in Jack Powell's ear. It wasn't fair, she raged, stomping from one end of the kitchen to the other.

And when another part of her responded: *Life isn't fair,* it only fueled her anger.

Beth began refilling the ketchup jars, wiping off the lids. And she instructed herself to calm down. She'd never felt like this before, so helpless and so powerful at the same time, and she didn't know what to do with it, or how she was supposed to get herself under control.

Maybe deep breaths.

Counting to ten . . . or a hundred.

Closing her eyes, sitting down, forcing her body to chill.

It all might have worked—but instead, she tightened her grip on the ketchup bottle, and then, without thinking, flung it across the room. It shattered against the wall, spraying glass through the air and leaving a garish smear of red dripping down the stained tile.

Beth should have felt horrified or panicked, afraid of herself—or for herself.

But she didn't.

She just felt better.

# chapter

## 10

Reed was all about avoiding the hassle. School sucked, but it's not like there was anything you could do about it, right? So he floated along, attending the occasional class, laying low, sneaking out for a smoke when it all got too much. He stayed under the radar. That would have been his motto, if he'd ever bothered to formulate one.

That, also, was too much effort.

So when they pulled him out of class, he was stumped—and also a bit stoned, which wasn't helping matters. He hadn't done anything. He never did anything. So why haul him down to the vice principal's office and stick him in front of the administrative firing squad?

Best not to speak until spoken to. More words to live by.

So Reed slouched in the low-backed wooden chair and stared at them: the principal, the vice principal, that French teacher all the girls were so hot for. They didn't scare him.

And then his father stepped into the office.

Shit.

"If you admit what you've done, I may be inclined to go easier on you," the vice principal finally said.

He'd done nothing, so he said nothing. And he tried not to look at his old man.

"Mr. Powell found the evidence," the vice principal continued. "You can't just weasel out of this one, Mr. Sawyer. Just tell us why you did it. And who helped you."

Reed laced his fingers together and put them behind his head, sliding down in the chair. He didn't have to speak out loud for them to receive his message: *Get to the point.*

"Does this look familiar?" Vice Principal Sorrento dropped a can of spray paint onto the desk. "Mr. Powell received a tip that led us to search your locker. Imagine our surprise when we found a number of these." He pursed his lips, as if it pained him to continue. "It's obviously what you used to doctor the billboard."

"I don't know anything about that." Damned if they were going to pin that lame stunt on him. As if he'd waste his time. If Reed wanted to say something, he'd say it—he wouldn't need to hide behind an anonymous prank. And if he had nothing to say, he'd shut up.

"Are you denying that we found these cans in your locker, young man?"

Reed snorted. "For all I know, you found them up your ass."

"If they're not yours, perhaps you have an alternate explanation to offer?" the principal jumped in, before Sorrento could lose his shit.

Reed shrugged.

"Maybe you've been framed, is that it?" Sorrento suggested sarcastically. "Someone's out to get you, right? And who might that be?"

Reed shrugged again. "For all I know, it was you."

That's when his father spoke for the first time. "That's enough! For God's sake, boy, just tell them you did it and that you're sorry, and we can get out of here."

Reed was sorry, but only that the school had bothered to drag his father out of work for this. His father usually didn't care what Reed did—but he *did* care about missing his shifts. And, like everything else, this would somehow become all Reed's fault.

He would have been happy to speed things along, even if it meant sucking it up for a parental lecture, but he wasn't about to admit to something he hadn't done.

*Bring it on,* he thought, staring at the vice principal. *You don't scare me.*

Sorrento couldn't threaten Reed, not with anything that mattered, because you could only threaten someone who cared.

"Mr. Sawyer, I hope you realize that your son is putting us in a very difficult situation here," Principal Lowenstein said. "I simply can't have this brand of . . . disruptive element polluting my student body."

Reed's father took off his cap and rubbed his bald spot, looking distinctly uncomfortable. Reed wondered what kind of memories this office held for the old man, who'd been a proud Haven High dropout, would-be class of '88.

"I understand, ma'am, you gotta do what you gotta do," Hank Sawyer said, and Reed winced, hating the way his father talked to the people who ran his life. "You wanna suspend him for a week or so, I'll put him to work, set him straight. You don't have to worry."

*Not his life,* Reed vowed to himself, not for the first time. *Not for me.*

"I'm afraid you *don't* understand me, *Mr.* Sawyer." It seemed to physically pain the principal to address Hank with even the barest term of respect. "If Reed here refuses to take responsibility for his actions—his very serious actions, I might add—we might be forced to take harsher measures. As I always say, if a student truly doesn't want to learn . . . well, I'm afraid sometimes there's just nothing we can do."

"I'm not sure I get what you mean," Hank mumbled.

But Reed got it. He wasn't as thick as people thought.

"She means if we can't settle this to our satisfaction— if we see no signs of . . . remorse, it may no longer be possible for Reed to attend Haven High School," Sorrento explained with a barely hidden smile.

Hank Sawyer looked dumbfounded.

Lowenstein looked apologetic—or rather, what she thought a suitably apologetic expression might be.

Sorrento looked triumphant.

Powell looked satisfied.

And Reed looked away. Whatever happened, he'd still have his job. He'd still have his band. He'd still have his buddies, and his stash.

There was nothing in this place he wanted or needed, so maybe Sorrento, for once in his miserable tight-ass bureaucratic life, was right.

Maybe it was time for Reed to go.

"I know I said I'd do the lab for you, but don't you think you should at least *pretend* we're working together?"

"Sorry, what?" Harper looked up from her doodles to discover her geeky Girl Friday had put down her beaker, turned off her Bunsen burner, and was waving the lab instructions in Harper's face.

"I *said,* how about you actually help me out here, before Bonner catches on?" The girl jerked her head toward the front of the empty room, where their robotic chem teacher was nominally supervising them.

Harper had cut class again today, unable to face Miranda across the lab table, but that meant a makeup lab—and *that* meant a big, fat zero unless she could find someone to do the work for her.

Enter Sara—or was it Sally? Sandra? whatever—a Marie Curie wannabe who always aced her labs and whose semester-long services could apparently be bought for the price of an outdated dELIA*s sweater and a setup with debate team captain Martin somebody the Third.

"Trust me, you don't want my help," Harper said, laughing..

"But it's easy," the brainiac argued. "If you just balance the equation and calculate the molarity of solution A, then you can estimate . . ."

Harper tuned out the droning. Back in the old days, with Miranda doing their labs, she hadn't been subjected to any of this chemistry crap; instead, Miranda had just measured and stirred and poured, all the while keeping up a running commentary on Harper's latest rejects or the possibility that the Bonner was naked under her ever-present lab coat.

Miranda had always known the perfect thing to say; she was never judgmental, patronizing, or—the worst crime, in both Harper's and Miranda's minds—boring. Harper had taken her for granted—and driven her away.

She got that now. Miranda and Adam were right: They'd been too good for her. Maybe she was lucky it had taken so long for them to realize it. And maybe she still had time to change.

"Thanks for your help, Marie, but I'll take it from here," she said suddenly, grabbing the lab instructions.

"Uh, my name is Sandra?" the girl pointed out, sounding slightly unsure of it herself. "And I'm not sure you want to do that. We're at kind of a delicate stage, and last time you—"

"I *said* I've got it," Harper said, accidentally sweeping one of the beakers off the table. Both girls jumped back as some of the solution splashed through the air.

Young Einstein pushed her glasses up on her face and began backing away. "Sure. Okay. No problem. I'll just get out of your hair then, uh . . . good luck!" She turned and raced from the room.

*No one's got any faith in me,* Harper thought in disgust. No one realized that she could be diligent and virtuous if she set her mind to it. Hadn't she managed to manipulate and connive her way to the top of the Haven High social pyramid? *That* took strategy, brains, and forethought. Compared to that, being a good person would be easy.

Harper sighed. Okay, maybe not easy. But it wasn't impossible; she was just out of practice. Whatever Miranda and Adam thought, she had it in her. She'd prove it to herself, and then she'd prove it to them. "Okay, what've we got here?" she mumbled.

*Step 3: Combine 10 ml of your titrated acid solution with 10 ml of water. Record the pH.*

What had Marie Curie Jr. said about balancing the molarity and calculating the equation of the solution? Or was it estimating the equation and balancing the solution? And what was a titrated acid, anyway?

Harper threw down the work sheet. She didn't need to get a perfect score on her first try, right? The important thing was making it through the lab on her own. So all she needed to do was concentrate and—

*CRASH!*

Oops. Hopefully that wasn't the beaker of titrated acid that had just smashed to the floor.

"Everything all right back there, Ms. Grace?" the Bonner asked nervously, too nearsighted to see for herself.

"Just fine, Ms. Bonner," Harper chirped. "Don't worry."

Harper picked up something that might or might not have been her titrated acid solution and dumped some into the remaining beaker. Then she spotted a test tube filled with a clear liquid. Marie must already have measured out the water; now, all she had to do was dump it in and . . .

A huge puff of smoke exploded out of the beaker, blasting past Harper before she had the chance to move out of the way. "Ugh," Harper moaned in alarm, "what's that—?"

The Bonner looked up in alarm, wrinkling her nose as the stench wave hit her. "Harper!" she cried, pinching her nostrils together and backing toward the door. "What did you do?"

"I don't know!" Harper waved away the foul greenish smoke, trying to hold her breath and escape the noxious combination of rotten eggs and raw sewage. She dumped the beaker into the sink, grabbed her backpack, and ran out of the room, joining the Bonner in the hallway.

"Oh dear oh dear oh dear," the Bonner was muttering to herself. "I'll have to contact the principal, I'll have to have the room fumigated, I'll have to—" She caught sight of Harper, or rather, caught *scent* of Harper. "Smells like we'll have to get *you* fumigated too," she said, stepping away.

Harper took her hand away from her nose and breathed in deeply, her eyes widening in horror. She smelled like she'd gone swimming in a toilet.

The Bonner shook her head sadly and pulled her lab coat tighter around herself, as if it would offer some protection from Harper's cloud of stench. "Ms. Grace, I'm afraid I'll be forced to give you a zero on this lab."

Harper looked down at her soiled clothes and back at the lab-turned-toxic-waste dump, took a big whiff of her new eau de sewer, and nodded. "Zero sounds about right," she muttered. Apparently, these days, that's all she was worth.

When Kane had coaxed Miranda out for a post-detention aperitif, he hadn't intended a torture session at the Nifty Fifties diner. But when Miranda had suggested it, her face flushed with pleasure, he'd said yes almost instantly.

Not that there weren't plenty of good reasons to stay away from the diner, even above and beyond those the local health inspector published in the town paper every year. He could have cited the watery milk shakes and five-alarm chili, aka heartburn-waiting-to-happen. He could have reminded Miranda of the grating Chuck Berry anthems piped through tinny speakers, punctuated by scratches, squeaks, and the high-pitched whine of a grimy waitress announcing "order's up." Then there was the burned-out neon, the scratched, faux-leather bar stools, the vintage movie posters peeling off the wall, and the Route 66 junk clogging the counter, longing for impulse buyers to give them a new home.

But all of those would have been excuses, skirting the truth of why he'd hoped never to set foot inside the dilapidated diner again. It was Beth's turf, and he didn't want to face her there. He'd spent one too many long afternoons lingering over a greasy plate of fries, waiting for her to finish her shift, and he could do without the flashback to happier days.

But when Miranda had raised the idea, he hadn't hesitated before agreeing, "Shitty Fifties it is." His own reluctance was reason enough to go; he wouldn't let Beth's presence scare him away from anywhere, especially one of Grace's few semi-tolerable dining establishments. Reluctance stemmed from fear, and fear was a sign of weakness, to be attacked wherever it appeared. Better to do it yourself, Kane believed, than wait for someone to do it for you.

He and Miranda kept up a steady stream of banter as they settled into a booth and waited for their food to arrive. She was so much easier to be around than most girls, neither boring nor demanding, just . . . there. Like one of the guys, only with a better ass.

"You sure you don't want some?" he asked, waving a spoonful of ice cream under her nose.

"You're a growing boy, Kane—I can't take food out of your mouth."

He shrugged and swallowed another mouthful of the flavorless vanilla.

"Not quite Ben & Jerry's?" she asked, grinning wryly at his expression.

She was okay, he supposed—physically, probably even a seven, thanks to her long, slim legs and model's body. The chest was a little flat for his tastes, but she compensated for it with a tight ass. Her long, thin face wasn't complemented by the long, thin hair—but it wasn't bad. It was the rest of her that brought the total package down to a five: the way she never quite looked you in the eye, the plain white T-shirts, boxy jeans, the fight-or-flight reflex on overdrive, and, most problematically, the way she seemed so content to fade into the background.

She was a fixer-upper, basically. The raw materials were all there. It would just take some effort—a project best saved for a rainy day.

Beth, on the other hand, was fully formed, and a perfect ten. She'd have to be, for Kane to be giving her a second thought. As Miranda longingly eyed the milk shake he had insisted she order—and from which she'd yet to take a sip—he eyed Beth. Her long, blond hair was pinned back from her face, and her full lips glistened with a see-through gloss.

He still wanted her, he realized. Despite everything, he missed her.

It only made him more determined to wash her out of his system for good.

"Waitress," he called loudly, "we need you over here." He'd sat in this section deliberately, knowing how much she hated to be watched at work. That was the thing about being in a relationship, he'd discovered: You learned people's weaknesses.

It was why he planned never to get ensnared in one again.

"What are you doing?" Miranda hissed, as Beth approached. She clucked her tongue. "Play nice."

"Do you need something else?" Beth asked thinly. "Or just the check."

"I need you to clean up this spill."

"What spill?"

True, the table was clean. He'd have to remedy that. Kane took a sip of his Coke, and then, with a slow and deliberate turn of the wrist, dumped it out all over the table. The sticky brown liquid spread across the metallic tabletop, spattering onto her white sneakers. "Oops."

Beth took a deep breath, then tossed a filthy dish towel in his face. "Clean it yourself."

"Excuse me?"

"Kane, drop it," Miranda said sharply.

He glanced at her in surprise, raising his eyebrows questioningly. *What? What did I do?*

"Can you, just for once, not be an asshole?" Miranda asked, as if genuinely curious to hear the answer.

"Now, where's the fun in that?" he drawled, waiting for the inevitable smile.

But Miranda's face was indecipherable, her lip twitching slightly, as if choosing between potential expressions. Finally, she settled on a scowl. "I'm going to the bathroom," she announced, standing up and throwing down her napkin. "I'll be back, maybe. Try to behave yourself."

She hadn't walked out on him, Kane thought with pleasure; he disliked melodrama of all kinds, unless he'd created it himself. But she hadn't egged him on, either, or sat there with an adoring look the way the bimbos all did, chastising him with their words while rewarding him with their eyes. No, the original go-along-to-get-along girl, Miss Gumby herself, had actually taken a stand—of sorts.

He could apologize later; for now, Beth still stood over him, fuming, and he found that he couldn't stop himself from pushing just a little harder.

"I know this isn't the finest of dining establishments," he drawled, "but didn't they bother to teach you that the customer is always right?"

"I guess you're the exception that proves the rule," Beth snapped. "I always knew you were special."

"Oh Beth, just give it up," he said, suddenly raising his voice to ensure that it would carry to the table of eavesdropping juniors a few feet away. "We're *not* getting back together."

"What?"

She was so smart in some ways—and so pathetically dumb in others.

"I'm glad it was good for you," he continued loudly, "but it just wasn't for me. I'm sorry—you're just . . . not very good."

"Shut up." Her pale face was turning a bright red. "Stop."

"You keep saying that, and yet you just keep coming back. It's a little embarrassing."

"*You're* embarrassing."

What a snappy comeback.

Kane smiled serenely and handed back the dish towel, now sopping with Coke.

"I'm serious about one thing," he said more softly. "Stop pretending this is all some game you can win."

"I thought everything was a game to you."

"That's because I know how to play." He gestured toward the giggling juniors who kept sneaking looks before turning back to their huddle and bursting into laughter. "As you can see. When you're a born loser, it's better to just stay out of the game altogether. Just a helpful piece of advice, from me to you."

"You—I can't—what—"

"Spit it out," he sneered, trying to convince himself he was having fun.

"Go to hell." And she picked up Miranda's untouched milk shake, gave him her sweetest Beth smile, and dumped it over his head.

It was juvenile, but effective—and very, very cold.

He smeared a finger across the icy goop sliding down his cheek, stuck it in his mouth, and sucked, hard.

It was sweet, but not as sweet as what came next. An overweight, under-showered man lumbered up behind Beth and, in a voice choked with anger, uttered the three little words that every bitter, milk shake–covered ex wants to hear:

"Manning? You're fired!"

Kaia hadn't known where to look, not at first. She didn't even know where he lived, she realized. It was just one of the many things she didn't know about him.

It should have been a warning, she thought now, disgusted with herself. She'd been so eager to believe in Reed that she'd ignored the possibility that his sleazy, pothead, criminal-in-training exterior wasn't just a veneer.

She still couldn't quite believe that someone who'd kissed her the way he did could have tormented the way he had. How had he touched her so gently, and then branded her a whore? It didn't seem possible, but the evidence didn't lie. They'd found the paint in his locker: two cans, both red, like blood.

As soon as she'd heard the truth, she'd gone looking for him. She'd searched the dingy Lost and Found, his father's garage, and Guido's Pizza, but had no luck at any of them.

Then she realized that she knew exactly where he'd be.

She drove slowly down the highway, savoring the roar of the BMW's engine and the clatter of the gravel kicked up by her tires, trying to enjoy the dusty billboards:

AIRSTREAM TRAILERS FOR SALE!

GET MARRIED QUICK—GET DIVORCED QUICKER!

LIVE! NUDE! GIRLS!

She was dreading the encounter, yet hungry for it, eager to finally have an end to the uncertainty and an outlet for her rage. She arrived at the mines, and his truck was pulled off onto the shoulder of the road, just as she'd expected. Reed was standing at the mouth of the abandoned mine as if wondering whether to disregard the fading DANGER signs and step inside.

"What's wrong with you?" she asked, keeping a few feet of distance between them.

"Excuse me?"

"Forget it. I don't even care. I just came here to tell you

to stay away from me." She didn't touch him, or look at him, just stood next to him, facing the gaping hole at the head of the mines. The industrial processing complex stood several yards away. This entrance must have been a remnant from an even earlier era, one of pickaxes and rickety wooden machinery. It had once been boarded up with plywood and barbed wire, but the wood had rotted away, and the torn, frayed strands of the jagged wire climbed haphazardly over the entrance like vines. It would be easy enough to slip inside.

"What the hell are you talking about?"

"I heard what they found in your locker," she snapped. "You think I'm too stupid to see what that means?"

"You think that crap was mine?"

"What else am I supposed to think?"

Reed shrugged. "Whatever. Do what you want. Get out of here. I won't follow you."

He began to walk away, toward the entrance to the mines. The dark, hulking mouth of the tunnel loomed over him. It reminded her of a carnival haunted house, but with no safeguards to stop the roof from crashing down.

"Where are you going?" she asked, grabbing his shoulder. "Are you crazy?"

"Maybe." He turned back to her. "What do you care?"

"I don't."

"Hey—" He grabbed her shoulders, and she felt a moment of panic but resolved not to let it show. "I don't know what's going on with you or what's got you so mad, especially when you're the one who . . . I know there's some other guy, and—"

"And that's it, right?" She tore out of his grasp and

started hitting at his chest. "I cheated on you, and that makes me a slut, right? A *whore*? Go screw yourself. You don't scare me." Her voice was rising, but she couldn't help herself. "Do you hear me? You. Don't. Scare. Me."

He grabbed at her hands, and she swatted him away until finally he grasped them both and held them still. "I don't want to scare you," he said softly, intensely. "Look at me. *Look* at me," he insisted as she stared resolutely over his shoulder.

Finally, Kaia gave in and met his dark eyes. She shivered, still feeling the irresistible pull to give in, to fall against him and forget herself. She leaned in, hating herself, but hating him more. Then she stopped, just before their lips touched. He was so close that when he spoke, she could feel the movement of his lips even before she heard his words.

"I need you," he whispered. "I need you to believe me."

*Remember the car,* Kaia told herself, *remember the flowers, and the photos.* She breathed in and out, aware only of his strong hands wrapped around hers, and the dark locks of hair framing his bottomless eyes. She wanted things to be different; but Kaia had given up on fairy tales long ago— you couldn't make something true just by wishing for it. You couldn't turn a frog into a prince just by giving him one last kiss.

"I'm sorry," she whispered back, pulling away. "I can't."

He didn't say anything as she walked away, nor did he follow. She got into the BMW and leaned her head back against the cool leather headrest. Maybe now it could finally be over.

Reed had turned his back on her, and was striding

toward the entrance of the mines. Kaia sat behind the steering wheel, one hand on the ignition key, one hand clenched into a fist, unable to stop watching as he swung one leg over the barbed wire, then another, then ducked beneath the rotted wooden boards and disappeared into the dark.

"Sorry about before," Kane said as they walked out of the restaurant together.

"Before? Oh, you mean when you pulled off that great magic trick, turning into a giant asshole before my very eyes?" But Miranda asked the question without rancor; she knew she should have been disgusted by Kane's treatment of Beth, and was a bit disgusted with herself for not caring more. Instead, she'd made excuses for him: He'd been hurt, was just lashing back—and the saddest thing of all was that the prospect of him still harboring feelings for Beth was what upset her the most. Someone else might have mistaken his cruelty for anger, but Miranda recognized it for what it was; and if he still felt that way about Beth, there seemed no hope he'd ever look in her direction. No matter how much time they spent together, it suddenly seemed likely that Miranda was only imagining the possibility it could ever be anything more. Just because you talked yourself into believing in something didn't make it true.

"Actually, I was apologizing for stepping on your foot back there," Kane said, laughing, "but let's say it covers the asshole thing too. And, since I spoiled our afternoon, let me make it up to you." He led her to the car and opened the door for her.

"And how are you going to do that?"

"A little fun in the sun," he said cryptically, getting behind the wheel and pulling out of the lot. Miranda wrinkled her nose in confusion, but said nothing as they followed a familiar route, finally pulling back into the school parking lot.

"Didn't you say something about fun?" she asked as they came to a stop.

"Trust me." He got out and went around to the back of the Camaro, pulling a basketball out of the trunk. Miranda gaped at him in horror.

"No. No way. Are you kidding me?"

"Stevens, I am about to do you the biggest favor of your life," he promised, grabbing her hand and pulling her toward the rickety outdoor court set up on the opposite end of the parking lot.

Miranda hated sports. She hated everything about them: the running, the jumping, the sweating, the terror when she caught the ball, the humiliation when she missed it. The last thing she wanted to do was subject herself to all of that in front of Kane, object of her deepest and darkest desires.

But he was tugging her along and giving her that boyish grin she couldn't resist. He was holding her hand.

"I'm not sure I see where the favor part comes in," she said skeptically as he began bouncing the ball against the concrete pavement. "Unless you're about to clue me in on how to get out of gym for the rest of my life."

"Better." He tossed the ball casually toward the basket, turning away a moment before it swooshed through the net. "Stevens, I'm about to show you the surefire way to any guy's heart." He grabbed the rebound and tossed it toward her; she hoped she didn't look like too much of an idiot when it slipped out of her hands and rolled away.

"*Basketball* is the key to any guy's heart?"

"Basketball, baseball, whatever—no guy wants some girlie-girl who's going to get all mushy when it comes to sports," Kane explained, chasing the ball and tossing it back to her. This time, she caught it. "Football works, too, though." A slow smile spread across his face. "Especially the tackling."

Miranda threw the ball toward the basket as hard as she could—it arced back down to the ground long before coming anywhere near the net. "So this is all for my own good?" she asked.

"Yup."

"You're just helping me out of the goodness of your heart?"

"Shocking, isn't it?"

"And it's got nothing to do with the fact that you missed practice today and you're just looking for an excuse to get out on the court?"

Kane stopped dribbling and turned to stare at her, an unreadable expression on his face. "You think you've got me all figured out, don't you?"

Miranda shrugged. "Pretty much."

Kane jogged over and handed her the ball. He placed both hands on her waist, turning her around to face the basket. Miranda tried to keep her breathing steady and ignore the fact that she could feel his breath on the back of her neck. He reached around her, arranging her hands into a shooting position while murmuring soft instructions in her ear.

"Like this . . . no, a little higher . . . use your right hand to balance it . . . bend your knees . . ." When she was set up exactly as he wanted, he stepped away, instructing her to freeze in position. It wasn't too difficult; Miranda hoped never to move again, the better to remember every place he'd touched her.

"Most girls wouldn't do this, you know."

"What?" she asked, forcing herself to stay focused on her bent knees and straight posture and *not* on Kane's reedy voice or laughing eyes.

"This, here. All of it."

Miranda suspected he'd have no trouble getting most any girl in school out on the court, especially if it meant some physical contact with Haven High's resident Greek god. But all she said was, "I'm not most girls."

"Tell me about it," he said as she launched the ball into the air, holding her breath as it sailed closer and closer to the basket . . . and bounced off the rim.

"Told you I suck." She rolled her eyes and began walking toward the sidelines, but he grabbed her, drew her back to the center of the court.

"Okay, you *do* suck," he agreed, retrieving the ball and slipping it back into her hands.

"Nice. Very nice."

"But you've got a great teacher." He moved behind her again, and this time, as he grabbed her arms, she leaned back, ever so slightly, so that her shoulders grazed against his chest. She could feel him breathing. "See? That was only your first try and you hit the rim. It's a start."

*Of what?* she wanted to ask, playfully but meaningfully. Of course she didn't have the nerve. So she closed her eyes, feeling his chest rise and fall, his voice soft in her ear, and let him guide her body into position. It didn't mean anything, she knew that. He didn't realize what it felt like, his fingers wrapped loosely around her forearms, caressing her hips, her lower back, her thighs—for him, this was just another day on the court.

But even though she knew it was silly, Miranda allowed herself a moment of let's pretend: *What if* he spun her around and pulled her into his arms, for real? *What if* this was all just foreplay, and the real game was about to begin? *What if* he wanted an excuse to touch her just as much as she longed to be touched?

And then he let go again and, perfectly lined up for the shot, she let the ball fly off the tips of her fingers. It sailed toward the basket, rolled around the edge of the rim, again and again, before finally tipping away and toppling to the ground.

She'd missed. Again.

But it was a start.

It was pitch black inside the mine. But Reed didn't need to explore. When he was a kid, he'd spent hours blundering around in the dark, holding a flashlight up to his head like an old-time miner. He could've gotten himself killed.

This time, he just stepped far enough inside the darkness to make everything disappear, then sat down, his back pressed against the cool, dank wall.

What did she want from him?

Why did he even care?

His father wanted him to confess, and had already made it clear that he'd throw Reed out of the house if he got expelled.

Then what?

Reed wished he could light up a joint, since that was the best way to drive the questions away. A few puffs and he could sink into the worry free zone and forget it all. But you didn't sneak into an old mine and light a match—not if you cared about staying alive.

There were other ways to forget. Reed closed his eyes—though there was no light to shut out—and leaned his head back against the wall. He could almost hear the sounds of an earlier time: pumping, clanging, chugging, grunting, rhythmic grinding of steel on steel. That was why he liked it here: The place was full of ghosts, and it was easy to imagine you were one of them, fading into the past, all your problems long solved, your decisions made, your life lived.

Reed knew he'd eventually have to get up, walk out, and *do* something. He couldn't just hide there in the dark, waiting for his problems to pass. But it was tempting to imagine the possibility, just for a while.

He'd never been afraid of the dark, just like he'd never been afraid of dying. As far as he was concerned, darkness was easy. Leaving it all behind was a piece of cake. The hard part came when you turned on the lights and had to face the day.

# chapter

## 11

Kaia wasn't sure she owed Powell an apology, and she hadn't decided whether she wanted to give him another chance or whether the time had come to make a clean break from both of the men in her life. All she knew was that she needed to see him, and didn't know why.

The uncertainty had driven her straight to his doorstep.

"Kaia, *ma chérie.*" He swung the door open before she had a chance to knock. "I've been expecting you."

The last time Kaia had been in the cramped bachelor pad—*every* time, in fact—she'd headed straight for the bedroom, which was large enough to fit Powell's sagging mattress and not much else. This time, she sat on the futon. It was burnt orange, inherited from the previous tenant. Powell squeezed in next to her, and Kaia willed herself not to inch away.

There was one question answered: She didn't want him back. His pathetic threats had twisted Kaia's attraction into an instinctive repulsion.

"I knew you'd be back," he leered, fondling a strand of her hair.

She slapped his hand away. "I didn't come here for that," she informed him.

"What, then?"

"It's over," she told him. She was certain now of what she wanted, but uncertain about too many other things— like why she'd felt so safe with Reed, even knowing what she knew, and why, sitting here on this familiar futon with her horny but harmless ex, she felt a shiver of danger.

Powell sighed. "Haven't we danced to this song before?"

"Don't be—"

"Cute. I know." He tried to put an arm around her, and she jumped up off the futon, unsure why she felt so jittery, but willing to trust her instincts. "What? Are you still going on about that stalking thing? I told you, not my style."

"No, I know it wasn't you . . ."

"And you can't seriously still think the Sawyer boy is a reasonable option—not after what happened yesterday."

"How do you know about—"

Powell shook his head, his eyes twinkling. "I was there when they tossed him out of school. Very sad case, that. So tragic to see a young man just throw his life away, and all on a nasty little prank."

Now Kaia sat back down again, taking Powell's hands in her own and trying to smile. This had all worked out a little too well, especially for him. "Jack, tell me something." She raised a hand to his temple and wound a finger around one of his chestnut hairs, curling it idly as she spoke. "How did you know about me and Reed, really?"

"I told you, *ma chérie*, I just knew. I could tell."

She leaned toward him, brushing her lips lightly against his cheek, trying not to gag on the overpowering scent of his cologne. "You were watching, weren't you? It's okay, you can tell me. It's kind of a turn-on."

"Well, since you put it that way . . ." Powell traced his fingers down the side of her face and began lightly massaging her neck. Kaia tried not to jerk away. Then his fingers closed down on her skin, pinching her shoulder. He pushed her away from him, holding her in place like a vise. "What kind of an idiot do you take me for? 'Oh, Jack,'" he simpered in imitation, "'tell me all about how you love to watch me when I'm alone, how you've been following me, how you love to see me weak and scared. Tell me everything, Jack, it's *such* a turn-on.' If you want to know something, Kaia, just ask."

"You took the photos," Kaia said. It wasn't a question.

"No point in lying now, is there?"

"And the car."

"Mea culpa."

"You planted the spray paint in Reed's locker," she realized, the pieces all falling into place.

"A master stroke," Powell preened. "And yet you waltz in here ready to toss me away anyway, still loyal to that piece of scum no matter what he does. 'Stand by my man' really doesn't become you, dear."

"You're going to fix it—you know that, right?" She couldn't let them throw Reed out of school, especially now. The memory of pushing him away the day before rose in her like bile. "You're going to get him out of trouble."

"Or what?"

It was funny. Yesterday, when she'd thought she'd learned the truth about Reed, she'd felt empowered. But now, confronting the real threat, it was all she could do to force herself not to flee. "Or I sic my father on you. At school, it may be your word against mine, but if Daddy Dearest finds out that some perv has laid a finger on his darling daughter, what do you think he'll do?"

"Come at me with a baseball bat?" Powell sneered. "I'm trembling."

"Come at you with a team of lawyers," Kaia corrected haughtily. "Get you fired, deported, jailed—he'll get whatever he wants. He's just like me that way."

"Is he really ready to drag his baby girl's name through the mud?"

"Wouldn't be the first time. Though I doubt he'll have to, once his team figures out how you ended up in Nowheresville, USA, in the first place. We all know it wasn't by choice. What are you willing to do to keep that skeleton safely hidden in the back of your closet?"

Powell flinched, and Kaia suppressed a smile. Her hunches were never wrong. Jack Powell had obviously stuck his hands somewhere they didn't belong—and gotten burned.

"You really care about this loser so much?" he asked.

"I think the real question is, do you?" Kaia stood up. "Are you willing to risk it all, just to screw with him?"

"I'd rather screw with you," Powell said. "It would be a much more pleasant way to handle this. You stay here with me now, and in the morning, I'll smooth things over for your little playmate."

Kaia darted her eyes toward the bedroom. "You're suggesting . . . ?"

"Don't play coy, *mon amour.* You know exactly what I'm suggesting. Just think of it as—what's that they say here? 'One more for the road.'"

It would be nothing she hadn't done before . . . and it *would* be a much easier way of getting Reed out of trouble than involving her father, who was sure to make a huge deal out of everything, but—

Even the thought of touching Powell again filled her with revulsion. She couldn't whore herself out like that, even for Reed.

"Thanks, anyway, but I'll pass." She grabbed her purse from the couch, but he curled his fingers around it as well, suddenly yanking it toward him and pulling her off balance. His other hand clamped down on her wrist and pulled her back down to the futon, onto his lap.

He leaned over and kissed her, mashing their lips together and thrusting his tongue against her teeth, which were gritted together so hard, she thought they might snap.

"I *told* you to be nice to me," he growled, his breath sour and hot on her cheek. "I gave you every opportunity."

They wrestled for a moment, Kaia squirming and pulling, Powell's hands locked tight on their prey, his muscles—the ones she'd so admired, compact, but like steel—forcing her down on her back, knocking the back of her head against the metal bar of the futon, pinning her arms behind her head.

"One more for the road," he repeated as an unfamiliar sensation swept through her. Panic. "I think I deserve that much."

Adam did his best to behave himself at basketball practice—but once practice ended, he was ready to step out of bounds. Forget trying to earn back a certain someone's trust—he was done with women.

Correction: done with relationships. They'd done nothing but cause him pain, and all because he'd been thinking of other people when he should have been thinking about himself. He'd been slow to learn his lesson, but he'd learned it well.

Look out for number one—and right now, number one wanted some fun. Lucky for him, practice had been pushed back two hours since half the team was stuck in detention all afternoon. That meant missing dinner—but it also meant sharing the court with the cheerleaders. And now that he was back on the market, he was already their top priority.

*Time to make someone's day,* Adam thought. The inner voice, cocky and cruel, didn't sound like him. It sounded like . . . Kane. So much the better, Adam resolved. Kane was happy. Kane didn't lie awake nights cursing the way his life had turned out. And Kane, his only previous competition, was mysteriously absent from practice.

*More for me.*

As the coach blew the final whistle, Adam scooped up the ball and dribbled it down toward the bouncy bimbos, who had just finished their last tumbling routine. He heard a few hoots of encouragement from the guys before they headed into the locker room.

"Adam, you were playing so great out there today!" one of the new cheerleaders gushed. She was cute, with an almost frighteningly wide grin, and seemed vaguely familiar.

"Totally awesome!" another chimed in. She, too, seemed familiar, but he couldn't place her. "We almost screwed up our cheers because we were so busy watching you. Oh—" Her face turned red, and she burst into giggles. "I mean . . . we were watching the team."

It was the "we" that gave it away. Individually, they had cute but totally forgettable faces. Together, Adam would know them anywhere as the joined-at-the-hip sophomores who'd been following Harper around all year, worshipping at the feet of their goddess of cool. Harper claimed to detest them, and refused to learn their names, instead, dubbing them Mini-Me and Mini-She. Adam had always suspected that she loved the attention they lavished on her, vapid and giggly as it might be. They were her clones, her property—

They were perfect.

"Glad you liked the show," Adam said. *Smile*, he instructed himself, struggling to dig up the flirting skills he'd once had, before Beth. His mother had always told him he was a charmer—though she'd never made it sound like a good thing. He'd put that part of him up on a shelf somewhere for two years, but now it was time to dust it off, get back in on the action. "But you know, it's a team effort."

"Oh, the team would be nothing without you!" Mini-Me gushed. (Or was it Mini-She?)

"You're the *star*."

Adam sighed. Something about this felt wrong. *You're just out of practice*, he assured himself. After all, he'd thrived on this kind of attention for years before meeting Beth; there was no reason he couldn't turn back the clock and enjoy some meaningless fun. Or, at the very least, there was no reason he couldn't go through the motions and pretend he was enjoying himself—sooner or later, it would have to turn into the real thing, right?

"So . . . I guess since you girls go to all the games, you must see all our mistakes," he said, flashing a modest smile.

"No way!" Mini-She protested.

"You guys rock!" Mini-Me swung her pom-poms in the air, as if that should decisively settle the point.

"Still, I bet you could give me some pointers—you know, as objective observers," Adam said. "How 'bout I treat you both to some pizza and you can tell me what you think?"

"Us?" the Minis gaped at each other.

"*You* want to take *us* out?"

"*You* want to hear what *we* think?"

"Now?"

"Both of us?"

Adam nodded. Two girls—double your pleasure, double your fun, right?

(*This isn't you,* a small voice inside him pointed out. *Shut up,* he told it.)

"I'll go get changed and meet you back outside the school in fifteen minutes, okay?"

They nodded, too dumbstruck to say anything. Then, simultaneously, they turned and raced toward the girls' locker room, ponytails and pom-poms flying out behind them.

Adam trudged back toward his own locker room and

tried to think eager thoughts. But all he could think of was the looks on Harper's and Beth's faces if they saw what he was doing.

Beth would be disappointed.

Harper would be disgusted.

By the time he'd showered and changed, Adam was both—but it was too late to back out now. He wasn't the kind of guy who made a date and disappeared, even if it was a date his kind of guy should never have made in the first place.

They were already there waiting for him when he pushed through the front doors, each dressed in a tight-fitting skirt he was sure he'd seen Harper wear and discard a few months earlier.

"We were afraid you'd changed your mind!" Mini-Me chirped, her face lighting up when she spotted him.

"Ready to go?" he asked weakly. Mini-Me linked her arm through his.

"Three cheers for pizza!" Mini-She squealed, and grabbed his other arm.

Too bad Adam had lost his appetite.

Beth fidgeted in her seat by the corner of the stage, fuming. When the principal had asked her, as a special favor, to participate in the governor's assembly even though her speech hadn't been chosen, she'd figured it was a decent enough consolation prize. Some prize.

It turned out that "participate" had meant "introduce Harper and tell the school what a wonderful girl she is."

Upon realizing that, Beth had been too horrified to back out—she'd just frozen, bobbing her head up and down in response to the principal's babbled comments about poise and eloquence.

There wasn't enough poise in the world to pull this off, Beth thought, glancing to her left, where Harper was playing with a long thread fraying off the pocket of her jeans. The principal had insisted on having a run-through before the main event—and it wasn't like Beth had anywhere else to be. After all, work wasn't an issue anymore.

*Get out,* her manager had said. *Take off your uniform, leave your time card, and get out.*

All those months of sucking up to him, with his bad breath and greedy comb-over, all those late nights and double shifts, all wasted in a single, fatal failure of her impulse-control system. She'd trashed everything just because Kane Geary couldn't leave her alone and, for once in her life, she couldn't just grin and bear it.

Part of her believed it had been worth it, just for the look on his face—at least, the patches of his face visible beneath the dripping milk shake. But the other part of her knew she needed the job: for her family, for college, for keeping herself on track, and sane.

Still, it had felt good.

"Beth?" the principal called. "You're up."

"Good luck," Harper whispered.

"What's that supposed to mean?" Beth snapped.

"Just . . . good luck," Harper said with no trace of a smile. "I'm, uh, sure you'll be . . . great."

Beth stared at her, waiting for the punch line, but there wasn't one. Harper had never said a friendly word to her—not without an ulterior motive—and there was no reason to think she'd start now. "Don't talk to me," she hissed. "I don't want to hear it."

Beth walked slowly toward the podium at the center of the stage, thinking that something was wrong here. It should have been Harper delivering the saccharine opening lines, forced to stroke Beth's ego and choke on her words. It should have been Beth welcoming the governor, awing the auditorium of students and faculty and media with her stunning prose.

For a moment, Beth wondered: If she tried hard enough, could she wake herself up to find that she'd fallen asleep in Adam's arms three months ago, and all this was just a bad dream, brought on by pre-SAT stress?

"Ms. Manning? Any day now will do," the principal said dryly.

If it was a nightmare, it wasn't ending anytime soon.

Beth unfolded the small sheet of paper she'd brought with her, a two-paragraph intro she'd jotted down the night before. She took a deep breath and faced the sea of empty seats. "Thank you, Principal Lowenstein. And thank *you*, Governor, for visiting Haven High School. We're all so honored to have you here." *Pause for applause,* Beth told herself. But she was just delaying the inevitable.

"I'm now pleased to introduce one of Haven High's most distinguished students, someone who deeply cares—"

Beth stopped. This was a joke. As if Harper Grace had ever deeply cared about anything except herself.

But they were just words, she reminded herself. Lies, yes, but not important ones. She just needed to talk fast and get it over with.

"Who deeply cares about the future of this school. As everyone knows, Harper Grace—"

She stopped again. She may not have had the nerve to speak the truth, but she didn't have the stomach to tell the lie.

"Are you okay, Beth?" Harper called from the side of the stage. At the sound of her voice, Beth only felt weaker.

Principal Lowenstein walked over to the podium and put a hand on Beth's shoulder. She flinched away. "Is everything all right?"

No.

When was the last time the answer hadn't been no?

"I'm just not feeling very well," she said softly. "I think . . . I think I need to go, if that's all right."

She fled before the principal had a chance to respond, and before she could see the jeering look on Harper's face.

Every time she thought she'd scored a point, it seemed like she just got kicked down into the mud again, trampled and humiliated. Everything she tried to do blew up in her face, while every move Harper made was flawless—and deadly.

Beth still had the moral high ground. She had all the principles in the world on her side. But Harper had the strength, the will, and the ruthlessness. Which meant Harper had the power, and maybe she always would.

Miranda had heard the rumors.

That Rising Sun Casino was a desert oasis, filled with bronzed guys and buxom blondes, high-roller tables and penny slots, drama, intrigue, adventure, a twenty-four-hour buffet and all the cocktails you could stomach. And they didn't card.

It seemed an unlikely setting for bacchanalia, Miranda thought, as the silver Camaro pulled into a space by the entrance of the casino. A few neon lights flickered on and off, and an old man lounged in the doorway smoking a cigarette. It didn't scream intrigue so much as infection.

But at least some of the rumors were true, Miranda discovered, as Kane held the door open and she walked down an aisle lined with withering potted palms. The cocktails were abundant, as were the buxom blondes ferrying them around the casino floor.

And indeed, they didn't card.

"You like?" Kane asked, sweeping his arms wide to encompass the place as if it were his handiwork.

Miranda couldn't help but wrinkle her nose. "It has a certain . . . charm." To her right, a line of older women looked up from their slot machines, their hands fixed on the levers with a death grip. (And they seemed determined to stay there until "death grip" became a literal description.) Eventually, having ascertained that neither Miranda nor Kane looked likely to infringe on their turf, they looked down again, back at the buckets of coins and spinning dials that always came up one short of the jackpot.

Kane laughed. "Never brought a girl here before," he admitted. "But, somehow, I thought you'd enjoy it."

Miranda flushed with pleasure. When he'd proposed the impromptu road trip after detention, she certainly hadn't worried about her curfew, or asked where they were going or when they'd be back. She'd just basked in the glow of his attention.

"So what's first?" he asked. "Blackjack? Slots? Maybe you want me to teach you a little poker?"

Miranda and Harper had been playing poker late into the night since junior high. They used M&M's and Vienna Fingers for chips, then ate their winnings. She shook off the memory and grinned up at Kane. "Please. Point me to the poker table. I'll kick your ass."

And she would have, too, if he hadn't pulled out a straight flush at the last second.

It was hard to tell when he was bluffing.

After a full circuit around the casino floor, it was clear: Kane couldn't lose—not at games of skill, not at games of chance.

They eventually ended up in the gift shop. Kane had declared they needed a souvenir to commemorate the occasion. "How about this?" He held up a teddy bear in a bright blue shirt reading I ♥ POKER.

"Congratulations. That may be the tackiest thing I've ever seen."

Kane clucked his tongue. "Oh, Stevens, you're not trying hard enough. Just look around us—this is a cornucopia of crap."

Miranda had known Kane for a decade, and had studied his every move for almost that long. She'd seen him sardonic, sarcastic, sullen, supercilious—but never quite like this. Never silly.

"Okay, then, how about this?" She lifted a pair of earrings, holding them up against her lobes; the bright orange and green feathers dangled so low, they brushed her shoulders.

"Gorgeous. Now all you need to finish off the look is . . ." He selected a heavy chain of oversize, garishly painted beads and fastened it around her neck. She shivered at his touch, and his hands paused. She looked up at him and, for a moment, it seemed like—

"Not my style," she said, ducking out of the necklace, and out of his reach.

*What is wrong with me?* Her heart was pounding, her breaths too fast and too short, and she backed up a step, almost knocking over the shelf of commemorative shot glasses. "Careful, Stevens." He took hold of her arm to steady her. "You break it, I buy it."

*Breathe,* she instructed herself. *This could be it.* But it was as if her body was rejecting the good luck as too alien for her system. She'd imagined this moment so many times, and now that it was here, she didn't know what she was supposed to do or say. She couldn't get her hands to stop shaking.

Probably, she was just imagining the sudden shift between them. Nothing was going to happen, she warned— or maybe reassured—herself. To Kane, she was just a buddy; why would he suddenly see her differently?

It must be the double vodka martini, she realized. It had made her forget herself.

She'd also forgotten that he was still holding on to her arm. Or perhaps he'd forgotten to let go.

"Problem, Stevens?" He smirked, and it was almost as if he could tell what she was thinking.

"I'm fine," she claimed. "But the martinis in me seem to be a little clumsy."

"I don't think it's the martinis." He guided her toward the back of the gift shop, against a wall of "Guaranteed authentic!" Native American dreamcatchers. They were hidden from the rest of the store by a shelf of tourist guides to the Southwest. "I think you're nervous."

"Why would I be nervous? Were you playing with loaded dice?" she teased. "Think they're onto us?" She shook her head in mock disappointment. "I should have known you'd only gamble on a sure thing."

"You know me too well." He was close enough now that she could smell the alcohol on his breath. How drunk was he? she suddenly wondered. How much of this amazing afternoon was him, and how much—"That's what I love about you," he said softly.

"And here I thought you only loved yourself." She kept her voice hard and bright, hoped he wouldn't see how that word affected her.

Kane grabbed her hands and pressed them to his chest. "Stevens! You wound me! Here I am trying to be all sensitive and all you have for me are insults and innuendos?"

He was joking—or, at least, she hoped he was. Miranda had a nasty habit of blurring the line between flirtatious banter and cutting dismissals. But this time, she felt relatively safe, and so she played along.

"So sorry, Kane," she gushed fakely. "However can I make it up to you? I'll do anything!"

"Anything?" He arched an eyebrow.

"Anything your devious little heart desires."

He smiled then, the same smile he'd given her at the poker table just before laying down his hand: *I win, you lose.*

"Then kiss me already."

And there, between the dreamcatchers and the tourist guides, swaying to the scratchy, easy-listening remix of an old Céline Dion song, Kane gently cupped her chin in his warm hand, tipped her face toward his, closed his eyes, and slowly brought their lips together.

Technically, it wasn't her first kiss—but, in a way, it was. Because always before, it had been about the mechanics: the teeth scraping, tongue swirling, saliva swishing. Miranda had always focused on her breathing and where her hands should go, on the sucking and popping noises her lips made, silently wondering, *Is this it? Can this be all there is?*

Now she had her answer: no. That was nothing. This was—this was Hollywood, this was *Gone With the Wind*, Kirsten and Tobey hanging upside down in *Spider-Man*, Elizabeth and Mr. Darcy in *Pride and Prejudice*. This was every amazing kiss she'd ever imagined, with sparks and fireworks and a shock of pleasure exploding through her body.

This was Kane Geary caressing her cheek, sucking on her lip, moaning softly, pressing her against the gift shop wall. And this was her, forgetting herself, and how she might look or whether she was doing it right, forgetting to worry about what it might mean, how far it might go, if they'd be caught.

This was pure. This was passion.

And, most impossible of all—

This was real.

Would everyone in the audience hate her, Harper wondered, gripping the sides of the podium. Would all those hundreds of faces watching her be hoping for her to fail, or maybe just wondering what the hell she was doing up there in the first place?

She'd tried to stay true to her resolution to be a better person. She'd even been nice to Beth, much as it had twisted her stomach. It hadn't done much good. Beth didn't want her to change, that was obvious; Beth wanted her to be the unredeemable bitch, someone she could blame all her problems on, so she wouldn't have to take a closer look at herself. Harper knew the feeling.

But Harper couldn't avoid looking at herself now. She looked out at the sea of empty chairs and grew certain that tomorrow's audience would see right through her surface, down to her rotten core. And what was her reward for all this self-examination? Clammy hands, sweaty brow, pounding heart, lockjaw. She didn't need *Web*MD to diagnose herself. It was a textbook case: stage fright.

Harper fixed her eyes on the top line of the speech. She opened her mouth.

Out popped a squeak, and nothing more.

Her lips were dry, and her tongue suddenly felt too large for her mouth. She needed water. She needed air— in bigger and bigger gulps.

She needed to get away.

"Ms. Grace?" the principal asked, probably suffering from her own case of déjà vu. "Everything all right?"

*Yes,* she tried to say. *It's fine.*

But nothing came out.

And Harper Grace didn't do speechless.

*There isn't even anyone watching,* she told herself angrily. But it didn't seem to matter. It was all those empty seats, all that space, all the pressure—

"I have to get out of here," she mumbled, finally able to speak now that she'd given up the fight. She left the copy of the speech on the podium, waved weakly at the principal, and ran off stage, feeling sick.

She'd always been proud to be Harper Grace, with the distinguished name and the impeccable rep—everyone wanted her life.

They could have it.

*Is this what it feels like?* Kaia asked herself dimly in the small, faraway place she'd retreated to in her mind. She pushed Powell away, twisted, turned—but wasn't it all a bit half-hearted? Wasn't there a piece of her wondering, *Is this really happening?* She couldn't believe, couldn't force herself back down into her body, where it would be real. It seemed like something she was watching on TV, like one of those inter-changeable Lifetime movies where the damsel always finds herself in distress. As if the scene would play out the same way no matter what she did.

Kaia had always thought that, in a real emergency, life would be clearer, the picture sharper. You wouldn't coolly wonder whether those self-defense classes had been a waste of money, you wouldn't be as cold and calculating as you were in everyday life. You would recognize the need to act. Instinct would take over.

You wouldn't wonder, *Should I scream? Will that seem foolish? Am I overreacting?* You wouldn't wonder, coldly, curiously, *What's wrong with me? Why don't I scream?*

And then she heard the low purr of the zipper, felt it scrape against her skin, and then she did scream. She stopped thinking and wondering because it *was* real—he was on top of her, heavy, unmovable, and she screamed and spit and bit and tore at him, and still his hand clenched both her wrists and forced her arms down though her muscles screamed in pain, and when she slammed her forehead up into his, he barely moved, barely noticed, so intent was he on holding her down, shifting into position, wriggling out of his khakis with one hand while gripping her wrists with the other—

Her knee came up, hard. And connected. He dropped her wrists, grabbed his groin, doubled over with a soft sigh, and she sat up and punched him in the Adam's apple. Twice, for good measure. Grabbed her purse—not her shirt, though, because he was on top of it, half sitting, half lying on the futon, grunting with pain. But before she could escape, he pulled himself up and lunged toward her. She darted away, but not fast enough, and he slammed her against the wall, the edge of the futon digging painfully into her lower back. He grabbed her hair, tugged her head back, his laughter hot against her skin.

One hand pinned between their bodies, her other flailed behind her, waving wildly through the air, then fumbling across the coffee table until she felt the head of his tacky marble copy of Rodin's *The Thinker.* It was solid and heavy in her grasp, and in a smooth arc she hoisted it into the air and slammed it into the back of his head.

There was a surprisingly quiet thud, and he fell limp against her, the small statue slipping out of her trembling fingers and crashing into the floor. A splash of blood lit up the stone face.

Kaia pushed Powell's inert body away, and it toppled to the floor, facefirst. She didn't check to see whether he was breathing, or wipe the blood off the statue or her finger-prints off the doorknob. She didn't cry, didn't scream, didn't hesitate.

She just left, fumbling with the lock, slipping out the

door and stumbling on her way to the car. She pulled out of the driveway fast, without looking, and sped down the road into the darkness, away from town, away from people, turning up the radio and rolling down the windows to drown the night in cold air and loud music.

She blew through three red lights and hit open highway before realizing: She had nowhere to go.

# chapter

## 12

"Hello?"

At first there was no sound on the other end of the line, then a harsh, rasping breath. And another. "I'm hanging up now," Reed warned, and was about to, when—

"Wait. Reed, please . . ."

"Kaia?"

It was her, unmistakably. And yet somehow, not her— not cool, contained, a voice dripping icicles.

Reed was stoned, and had been zoned out for hours lying on his bed, strumming along to an old Phish album. But through the haze, he began to feel the beast creeping toward him. Trouble. But was she in it, or looking to cause it?

"Kaia, what is it?"

"I shouldn't have . . . I didn't mean—"

"What's going on? What do you want?" *She's just mocking you,* he told himself. Nothing between them had been real, why should this be anything but a cruel joke?

But she didn't sound cruel. She sounded . . . broken.

"It's all my fault."

"What is?"

No answer.

"Kaia?"

"Kaia?"

Dial tone.

Another mistake. Kaia threw down the phone, cursing herself. She couldn't do anything right.

*Great idea. Call Reed for help. Throw yourself on his mercy.* It was almost as brilliant as going to Powell's house in the first place.

She was shivering.

So she pulled off onto the side of the road. No longer afraid of jackals or coyotes, or whatever lost and angry souls might be wandering the desert at night. What was left to fear?

She had no shirt. It was cold, a cloudless winter night, and she was curled up in the front seat of the Beamer, her cheek pressed against the smooth leather, wearing only her jeans and a black bra.

She wasn't crying. She must have been, at some point—her face was wet, sticky against the leather seat. But she couldn't remember. Could barely remember how she'd gotten there. The night was fading, the details blurring. She remembered only shards of moments: his hands on her wrists. The sound of the zipper. His body, limp and still. The blood. Driving faster and faster, the top down and the frigid air burning her face, roaring in her ears. Reed's voice as she hung up the phone.

*I have nowhere to go.*

*I have no one.*

The road was dark, the only traffic an occasional truck thundering by.

She could get out of the car, stick out her thumb. Someone would pick her up, take her as far away as she wanted to go, leave everything behind. And, after all, there was nothing to leave.

Or she could turn the key in the ignition, drive back to her father's house, slip inside and tear off her clothes, immerse herself in a scalding shower, cleanse herself of it all. Wash away his touch from her skin.

But instead she got out of the car, walked over to the highway emergency phone. She couldn't use her cell, not for this call. She leaned against the cool steel, fingers hesitating over the receiver.

He didn't deserve her help.

And maybe it was already too late.

But she lifted the receiver and, in a dull monotone, gave out the necessary information. No names, no circumstances, nothing that would connect her to the sordid mess. Just an address. Just, "Hurry."

And when the ambulance arrived? They'd find her all over the apartment, wouldn't they? Her shirt, her fingerprints, her hairs . . . his blood. If he woke up, who knew what he'd say. And if he never did . . .

She crawled back into the car and wrapped her arms around herself for warmth. She was so tired. Cold. Finished. Later there'd be decisions to make, consequences to bear. But for now, she couldn't. Couldn't go home, couldn't go to the cops, couldn't disappear on the open road. She was tired of fighting, of moving. She just wanted it all to stop. Just for a while, just long enough that she could get her bearings.

Long enough that she could stop trembling.

She was frozen, unable to do anything but curl up in a ball in the front seat, hug her knees to her chest, close her eyes against the darkness surrounding her.

She was spent.

She was tearless.

And she was on her own.

Miranda was grounded for two weeks.

And she'd never been happier.

When she'd strolled—more like floated—in the door at half past ten, her mother was waiting. Miranda had forgotten to pick her sister up after dance class, had skipped dinner, had disappeared without a word, had apparently worried everyone half to death.

She'd just smiled through her mother's tirade, and her father's gloomy silence. She'd ignored her sister's pestering questions, waiting impatiently for the moment she could flee upstairs, shut herself in her bedroom, and relive the day, minute by minute.

She climbed into bed without changing out of her clothes, at first not wanting to admit that the day had officially ended. But then, thinking better of it, she wriggled out of her shirt and jeans and kicked them onto the floor, relishing the feel of the comforter against her bare skin. It reminded her of Kane's hands.

She could still remember everywhere he had touched her. When she closed her eyes, she imagined the pressure of his fingers on her hip and the light, tickling touch of his nail tracing its way up her back, down her collarbone. She lay in bed replaying it, lightly touching her own lips, as if to evoke a shadow of how it had felt.

She imagined what it might be like to have Kane lying in the bed with her, his strong arms wrapped around her and his chest pressed against her naked back. Would she lie on top of his arm, she wondered. Or would that cut off his circulation? Would he instead tuck one arm under the pillow beneath her head, use the other one to pull her close, and twine his fingers through hers as they both drifted off to sleep?

Miranda had never shared a bed with anyone, unless you counted family vacations when she and her sister squeezed together on the lumpy cot next to their parents' bed. So she was unsure of the logistics.

But now, finally, she could at least be sure of what it felt like to have her body come alive at someone else's touch.

They had left the casino and wandered away on foot into the desert, where they had explored each other. After years of worship from afar, Miranda had been certain she'd known every inch of Kane, but she'd been wrong.

They had done little more than kiss before Miranda had gotten nervous and pulled away. She was fearful that would be the end of it, but not fearful enough to push forward in spite of herself. Kane had only smiled, nodded, stopped what he was doing, or about to do, and went back to the kissing—it seemed to go on for hours.

Suddenly, more than anything, she wanted to call Harper. In her dream scenarios, the romantic night always ended with a triumphant call to Harper, who would shriek and then listen in disbelief as Miranda described every moment.

Even as they'd kissed, Miranda had at times found herself silently narrating, as if preparing herself to tell the story.

*I couldn't believe he was touching me,* she had thought, as Kane's tongue explored her mouth and her hands brushed his silky hair away from his face. *And I couldn't believe how natural it felt. Isn't that weird?*

She hadn't admitted it to herself, but she'd been talking to Harper that whole time. She had spent so many hours listening to Harper bleed details of her own innumerable conquests—and always, Miranda had listened, waiting for the day when she would have her own story to tell.

Miranda considered it. She even lifted the phone, touched each of the familiar numbers in turn, lightly, as if rehearsing. She needed to tell *someone* what had happened. Somehow saying it out loud would make it real and save her from the fear that when she woke up in the morning, all this would prove to have been a dream.

But too much had gone wrong between them.

So Miranda put the phone back down and rolled over on her side, throwing her arm around a pillow and pretending it was Kane. Like a warm blanket, she tucked the memory of him around her—the laughing look in his eyes, the current between them when he first put his hands on her chin, when she knew for certain that everything was about to change.

*Then kiss me already,* she whispered to herself. She didn't need a witness. She remembered. Her body remembered. *It really did happen.*

It was their space.

It was sacred.

So what was he doing out there without Harper?

What was he doing out there with not just another girl—but *two*?

Harper pressed herself against the window of her dark bedroom, hating to watch yet unable to turn away, as Adam guided the girls to the large, flat rock—their rock—and lay down between them.

These weren't just any girls.

They were the sad, worshipful sophomores who wanted to have everything that Harper had—and now they were one big step closer to accomplishing their goal.

Harper could barely breathe as Adam took one of their hands. Her own hand made a fist, as if trying to clutch something that was no longer there.

The figures lay flat on their backs, side by side, and Harper wondered what they could be talking about, and whether Adam could be thinking about anyone but her. It seemed impossible; and yet, if he thought about her at all anymore, how could he bear to involve himself in something so sordid, in *their* place? How could he ruin the final thing they had between them and expect her to bear it?

Adam turned over to face Mini-Me, propping himself up on his elbow, and their heads moved toward each other. Mini-She rubbed his back, one of her legs crossing over and entwining itself with his. Harper thought she might throw up or pass out. But, instead, she just kept watching.

The scene unfolded in slow motion. Adam's face drew closer and closer to Mini-Me. And then, just before their lips touched, Adam froze and turned his head away, up, toward Harper's window.

*He knows I'm watching,* she realized. *He wants me to see.*

It was too dark to make out his face, but Harper imagined him to be sneering. He couldn't possibly see her, a dark figure in a dark window, but even so, it felt like their eyes were locked, and Harper willed him to see the person he needed her to be.

But he saw nothing but the darkened window, and after a moment, he looked away, back down to Mini-Me, and then he kissed her.

It was the perfect plan. But Beth didn't know if she had the nerve. It would humiliate Harper, dealing a crushing blow to that reputation she was oh so fond of. It would be the picture-perfect revenge for the way she had gone after Beth, systematically destroying everything that was important to her.

Beth held the small box in her hand and wondered: Did she have it in her? And could she do it right?

The old Beth had no experience with this kind of thing. She lacked the strategic-planning skills, the devious imagination. But the last few weeks had taught her a few things. She'd done a lot wrong, but this time, perhaps she'd finally get it right.

No one would be hurt. No property would be destroyed. And certainly no one would ever think to trace it back to kind, appeasing Beth, pure as the driven snow.

She hated the person she had been—the weak, meek girl who'd let anyone hurt her. But she missed her old self, as well, particularly her assumption that life was, despite what they say, fair. She had always believed that if she worked hard enough and long enough, she'd get what she wanted.

She'd been weaned on platitudes:

*Early to bed, early to rise . . .*

*A bird in the hand . . .*

*Revenge is a gift best served cold.*

That one was just as wrong as the rest of them—she didn't have the patience to wait for the perfect moment to arrive. She'd have to create it. It would, of course, have been preferable not to adopt the tactics of her enemies. It would be nice if turning the other cheek would get you anywhere in life. But it wouldn't. Harper had proven that.

Beth put the box in the outer pocket of her backpack. She wished that something would happen the next day that would allow her to forget it was there, and that the need for revenge would magically disappear.

She'd learned the platitudes from her father, who was full of them. His favorite: *If wishes were horses, beggars would ride.* And now Beth finally got it: Wishes weren't worth much. You couldn't just close your eyes and hope things would turn out right. You had to make things happen. Harper had taught her that, too.

Harper had been a good teacher this year—and, of course, Beth had always been an eager student.

Tomorrow would be the final exam.

She was ready.

"I didn't know who else to call," Kaia said apologetically, when Harper met her in the parking lot and handed her the shirt she'd requested. Kaia slipped it on. "Thank you."

"Dare I ask what . . ."

Kaia shook her head. "Better not to. Sorry I had to drag you out here. It's late, and—"

"Trust me, I could use the diversion," Harper admitted. She looked more closely at Kaia, who seemed normal on the surface—but that surface was somehow thinner, more fragile than Harper had ever seen it. She gestured toward the coffee shop they were parked in front of. "I don't know about you, but I could use a drink."

"No." Kaia ran a trembling hand through her hair. "I have to"—she looked at her watch, looked at the road, the car, anywhere but at Harper—"I just have to go."

"Not like this," Harper said firmly. "One drink. Just some coffee. We'll talk."

"I don't need—"

"Not for you," Harper said, only half lying. "For me. It's been a crap night. I could use some company."

As if too tired to fight, Kaia nodded. As they walked toward the door, Harper cautiously attempted to put a hand on Kaia's shoulder—in comfort, she thought. Kaia flinched away.

Inside Bourquin's, they nestled in two comfy, over-stuffed armchairs in front of a roaring fire. Each sipped a steaming cup of coffee, black.

"You sure you don't want to talk about it?"

Kaia shook her head again. "There's nothing to—"

"Come on."

"Okay, there's plenty to tell. But it's not like I'm going to—" Kaia stopped herself, and Harper recognized the look on her face. She'd worn it enough times herself, when she was about to say something catty and caught herself just in time.

"You talk," Kaia said instead.

"About what?"

"About anything, I don't care. I just want to . . . sample someone else's problems for a change. So just talk. What's going on with you?"

Harper couldn't stop herself from laughing.

"What?" Kaia asked, annoyed.

"It's just . . ." How to say it without sounding rude? Then again, who cared how she sounded? "My life is totally fucked up, everyone's gone, and—let's just say I never thought I'd be pouring out my problems to *you*."

Kaia lifted her mug in a mock toast. "Right back at you," she said, forcing a grin.

Harper sighed and slumped against her chair. She'd hated Kaia, once, and then they'd been cautious allies, brought together by circumstance. And now? Harper still didn't trust her. But she somehow felt that she knew her— or maybe that Kaia knew Harper. It was the one person she'd thought she'd never let see her vulnerable; but these days, Kaia seemed like the only one with whom she could drop the act.

"Where should I start?" she asked, rolling her eyes. "Adam's probably screwing some other girl in our back-yard, as we speak. Or two of them."

"Two girls? *Adam?*"

"Don't ask. Meanwhile, Miranda hates me. I've got to give this shit speech tomorrow and"—this time, her laugh-ter took on a twinge of hysteria—"turns out I've got stage fright."

•

"Well, at least that one I can help you with." Kaia dug through her purse and pulled out a tiny pink case, then opened it up and slipped two pills into Harper's hand.

"And this would be . . . ?"

"Xanax," Kaia explained. "Mother's new little helper. I snagged her stash before they shipped me out here. Take a couple before you go on. You'll be fine." She let forth an almost manic giggle. "I might have a few myself tonight."

Harper slipped the pills into her pocket and sank back into her seat. "One problem down. Too many to go."

"Feels like everything's closing in on you?" Kaia asked—and was that sympathy in her voice?

Harper nodded.

"Like you don't belong anywhere and you don't deserve to?"

She nodded again.

"Like everyone thinks they know you, but no one really does?" Kaia took a deep breath and surreptitiously wiped the corner of her right eye. "Feels like maybe you'd be better off if you just took off one night and never came back?"

"Run away and leave it all behind?" Harper asked, surprised—because she'd just been staring out the window imagining how good it would feel. "If only."

"Yeah. If only."

It wasn't their kind of thing. But it was a nice fantasy.

There was silence between them for a moment, comfortable enough that Harper found the courage to speak. "Have you ever . . . done something that you wished you could take back? You know, just go back in time, do it all over again, the *right* way?"

Kaia dipped her pinkie into the coffee mug and stirred it around the dark liquid. "Maybe."

"It just seems like it should be possible to fix things," Harper said, thinking of the look on Adam's face when he'd thought Beth was cheating on him. He'd crumbled, totally destroyed. All because he trusted Harper and she'd used that trust to ruin him. "One bad decision, one screw-up, that shouldn't be it. You shouldn't have to feel guilty forever, right? There should be *something* you can do."

"What, like atone for all your sins?" Kaia asked. She shook her head. "No. Sometimes, maybe. But sometimes . . ." She shrugged and closed her eyes for a long moment. "Sometimes you make the wrong decision and that's just . . . it. Everything changes. You can't go back."

"You really believe that?"

"I don't know if I really believe anything."

Harper nibbled on her lower lip. "I don't buy it," she said finally. "No second chances, no hope. That would be hell."

"Look around you," Kaia drawled, gesturing to the tacky, faded, over-stuffed and over-ruffled coffee-shop decor, the darkness that lay beyond them. "We're *in* hell."

"You really hate it here, don't you?"

Kaia shivered, though the coffee shop was almost overly warm. "More than anything," she said, almost too softly to hear. "More than you know."

Harper almost envied her. For Kaia, this was all temporary—she had somewhere to go back to, a happy memory and hope for the future to keep her warm. For Harper, this was it. Life in Grace was all there was. And she'd destroyed everything that made it bearable.

Kaia could dream about waking from the nightmare, going back to New York, moving on with her life.

But for Harper, this was permanent reality. There was no escape.

# chapter

## 13

"Check it. I think it's a secret service agent!"

"No way."

"No, look, he's got a wire leading up to his ear, and—"

"Nice try, but I think that's the janitor and his new iPod."

"Whatever, they must be here somewhere, since he's coming soon and—"

"Do you think there'll be a limo?"

"Or, like, a whole motorcade, with cops and shit?"

"Are those sirens? Adam, you hear that?"

"Adam?"

The pale cheerleader hanging off his shoulder was staring at him, waiting for some kind of answer. Adam didn't have one for her. He'd checked out. It was the only way he was making it through this whole big-man-on-campus act. Hanging out in front of the school with his buddies and three hot cheerleaders—one of whom, he'd discovered the night before, could do this thing with her tongue that . . .

It should have been awesome. A walk in the park. Instead, Adam was just zoned out, waiting for the bell to ring. If he was going to be bored and miserable, better to do it inside a darkened auditorium, where he could slouch in his seat and stare off into space, undisturbed. Better than here, where something was expected of him. He mustered a smile.

"Who cares?" he asked. "It's just the governor. Big deal. You aren't even old enough to vote."

"God, Adam, did you wave *hasta la vista* to your brain?" Mini-She gave him a gentle push, and he guessed he was forgiven for chickening out the night before after a couple kisses and a little over-the-sweater action. The whole double-your-pleasure angle had seemed so appealing in theory, but in practice, it had been too seedy, too sordid, too much.

And he had his doubts whether he could have handled even one of them; much as he hated to admit it, he was no longer into the one-night-only thing. Not that he'd admit it to the guys—or even to the girls, at least these girls. But he wanted something more, something better; he just didn't think he'd ever have it, not again.

"He's not just the governor," Mini-Me protested. She snuggled up again him, shoving Mini-She out of the way. "He's—"

"Here!" Mini-She shrieked, as the sirens blared and a full motorcade pulled up in front of the school. A fleet of Secret Service agents—and they didn't disappoint, dressed in black suits, sunglasses, cocking their heads to the side as commands issued from their earpieces—swarmed out of the fleet of black SUVs, pushing the gawkers back to create a perimeter for the figure emerging from the long black limo.

It was really him, he'd actually shown up. This was officially more excitement than Grace had seen since the eighties, when a movie crew had shown up, along with the requisite stars, trailers, and paparazzi—and then turned around and left a week later, sets built, extras hired, and funding vanished.

Adam waited to feel some excitement now that the big moment had arrived, but he felt nothing.

Let this be the biggest day in Haven High history.

So what?

For Adam, it was just another crappy day.

Kaia had driven all the way to school before allowing herself to consider whether or not to go inside. She'd scanned the local paper that morning, but there was no mention of a lone, British bachelor found unconscious in his apartment. Not that you'd expect the *Grace Herald*'s crack reporting staff to be on the case so quickly, not when said staff included only two reporters, one of whom worked from his "office" in the Lost and Found, and the other who restricted herself to items on gardening or fashion (preferably both). And though she'd lain awake all night, listening for approaching sirens, an impatient rapping at the door or even a late-night phone call, nothing had happened.

But Kaia had watched too much TV to be fooled into thinking she was in the clear. No, either Powell had woken up and elected not to tell anyone his twisted version of what had happened, or . . . he hadn't woken up at all. And maybe wouldn't.

Kaia couldn't decide which option she preferred. She wouldn't even allow herself to consider the question, since every time her mind strayed to the image of Powell lying there, his blood on her hands, she froze. And she couldn't afford to do that anymore, not while time was running out.

She could turn herself in, tell the truth, engage in the inevitable he said–she said, and hope things swung her way. She wasn't stupid—she knew that was the responsible thing to do, probably the smart thing to do. But she didn't feel very smart right now, and she'd never been a big fan of responsible.

She could waltz into school as if nothing had happened. Maybe Powell wouldn't remember, or wouldn't want to implicate himself, or wouldn't . . .

There were any number of ways this could come out okay and she could slip away from the whole thing unseen and unsuspected, if only she could get it together and put on the right show.

Or she could get back in her car, drive away, and make a new life for herself somewhere. It was the dream option—the impossible one.

The alternatives were all shitty, and so instead of choosing one, Kaia leaned against her car and pulled out her cell phone. There was one thing she was sure she needed to do, even if it was too late.

The voice mail picked up on the fifth ring, which gave Kaia enough time to collect herself and plan her words.

"Reed, I don't know if you want to hear this, but I need to tell you that I'm sorry. I was wrong, about everything. I'm sure you don't want to talk to me, but I need to talk to you, to explain and . . . just call me back. Please. Because I—" She paused, wishing she could bring herself to say more. "I'm sorry."

Showtime. The art room was serving as a greenroom for the presenters as they waited for the governor's entourage to settle themselves on stage and the student body to filter in.

Everyone was buzzing about Powell's "accident" the night before—thanks to a cryptic announcement, they all knew the dreamy French teacher was in the hospital, but for what, and from what, no one had any clear idea. Fragments had spread, phrases like "stable condition," "unforced entry," "open investigation," and "mitigating circumstances" floating through the grapevine courtesy of the sons and daughters of doctors, cops, nosy receptionists, and taciturn administrators. But no one had been able to piece together the full story, and no one could let it go, wondering: Was his pretty face still intact? Was it a bitter student? A jilted lover? Would French be cancelled? Would the perpetrator strike again?

Beth didn't care about any of it. She sat off to the side, alone at one of the large drafting tables, watching Harper across the room. Even from a distance, Beth could see her fingers tapping compulsively against the side, her knees jiggling, and, like Beth, she was steering clear of the huddling gossipers, locked in her own thoughts.

She looked nervous—*but not as nervous as I am,* Beth thought, clutching one of Kane's little yellow pills in the palm of her hand. She'd done some research the night before and decided one should be enough. And, according to her calculations, it was time. You had to give it some time to kick in, after all.

Beth felt like the room was watching her, but she

forced herself to take a deep breath and make her move. Two cups of coffee—the lukewarm instant crap courtesy of the faculty lounge. One for her—and one for Harper, with a little something *extra* mixed in for flavor.

Harmless fun, Beth told herself. That's all it was. No one would get hurt. Beth would get even.

"What are you staring at?" Harper asked sullenly, when she realized Beth was hovering over her desk. "Just thought you looked a little nervous," Beth said. "Thought this would help." She offered Harper a cup, making sure to give her the right one. Harper took a sip and put it down on her desk. Then she lifted it again and took a long gulp.

*There's still time,* Beth told herself. *I could knock over the cup before she drinks any more. I could forget the whole thing.*

"Thanks, I guess." Harper frowned. "As long as you're here, there's something I need to say."

Here it came. Beth steeled herself. "Yeah?"

"I . . . I wanted to tell you . . . well, about . . . I'm really . . ." Harper closed her eyes, and a series of expressions flickered across her face as if she was having an in-depth conversation inside her head. Then, all at once, she shook her head and her features relaxed into a familiar sneer. "Just don't screw up, okay?"

Forget turning back.

Beth smiled sweetly.

"Uh, thanks. Good luck to you, too." Beth backed away, retreated to the other side of the room—but she snuck enough glances to spot Harper downing the cup.

Beth checked her watch. It should take no more than twenty minutes. She couldn't believe she'd actually done it. She didn't know how she was going to wait.

At least this time she wouldn't have any trouble choking out her introduction. The more lovely things she had to say, the higher the audience's expectations rose, the harder Harper would fall.

Beth checked her watch again. Only a minute had passed. This was maddening. But there was nothing left for her to do now, nothing left to worry about.

All she had to do was wait it out—and then sit back and watch the show.

*Play it cool,* she'd told herself all night.

*Play it cool,* she'd insisted this morning as she wolfed down a bowl of cereal, eager to get to school to see him.

It was time to face facts: Miranda wasn't cool.

For years now, she'd borrowed cool from Harper, but that was over now. There was no one to tell her to keep her mouth shut and go with the flow. And there was no one to calm her down when Kane gave her a casual smile and quick wave as they passed in the hall—then kept going.

Was that it?

Was the whole casino trip a one-time deal? Or was he just keeping it casual, waiting to see what she wanted? Or—

Miranda couldn't sift through the possibilities like a rational human being. They buzzed around her, worst-case scenario piling on top of dreamscape, misery and ecstasy mixing together, and all the while, she was only half present to begin with, thanks to the chunk of her mind still dedicated to preserving the memory of his touch.

She hovered in the entryway of the auditorium, watching the students file in. No Kane.

No surprise—this wasn't his thing. When Miranda was

certain he wasn't there, she waited until the faculty had turned away to view the main event, then slipped out herself. She knew she'd find him in the parking lot, half hidden behind a utility wall, enjoying a cigarette.

She wasn't usually the kind of girl who could confront a boy—not someone like Kane, at least, who'd cowed her into silence for years. But the not knowing was even more overwhelming than her fear. So she spurred herself into action, and found him just where she'd expected.

One problem: She didn't know what to say. She hadn't planned that out, and could only hope that once she started, he would finish.

*This is a bad idea,* she warned herself, knowing that Kane wasn't the type to react well to being pressured; he *was* the type to do things without thinking and then hope never to speak of them again. *A very bad idea.* Still, she couldn't help but be a little impressed with herself. Who knew Miranda Stevens could ever be this brave?

"Hey."

He looked up and smiled as if he'd been expecting her. "Want a smoke?"

She waved away the pack. The way she was feeling now, the nicotine buzz would put her over the edge.

"So . . . get any flak when you got home last night? You know, for disappearing and—" She broke off at his laughter. *Stupid,* she berated herself. Of course *Kane* wouldn't get in trouble. He probably did this kind of thing all the time. *Nice job letting him know you're a loser with overprotective parents.* Still, she'd raised the subject. It was a start.

"So," she continued, in a small voice—her stomach was

clenched, and it felt like there was no air left in her lungs. "About last night . . ."

"Yeah, it was great, wasn't it?"

Miranda beamed, and some of the tension leached out of her.

"You know, if you were any other girl, I'd be so screwed right now," he continued.

"Why?"

"Oh, you know how it is—have a little fun and the girl gets all lame and clingy. Wants to know what it all means, where it's all going, crap like that." He took a long drag on the cigarette. "You know, girl stuff."

"Yeah," Miranda echoed weakly. "Girl stuff."

"But not you."

No, not good ol' reliable Miranda. No girl stuff here.

"You know me, and you're cool with it. And just because we had a great time yesterday, you're not, you know, freaking out and wondering where we'll go on our honeymoon."

*The Italian Riviera. Or maybe Tuscany.*

"It's what I've always liked about you, Stevens." He punched her lightly on the arm. Like she was one of his teammates. "You're not like other girls."

Uh, thanks?

Miranda clamped her teeth together, afraid otherwise they would clatter, and her lip would start to wobble uncontrollably as always happened when she was about to cry. She had to get away before it happened.

"Whatever, Kane." She forced herself to laugh. "As if I'd go all gooey eyed over you. Please. Could your ego get any bigger?"

"Well, I *am* working out." He offered her the pack of cigarettes again. "Come on, join me. It's rude to let someone smoke alone."

"Much as I'd like to join you on the road to lung cancer, I think I'll pass," Miranda said, trying not to meet his eyes. "I just came out here for a little fresh air. So that would kind of defeat the point." She checked her watch. "Anyway, I should probably get back inside. If someone notices I'm gone . . ."

"Who's going to—"

"Later, Kane." She had to leave now, fast, before he talked her into staying—and she so wanted to stay. Every moment she was around him was a moment of possibility. That *something* would happen. But it would kill her if something didn't.

And it wasn't going to.

"Suit yourself, Stevens." Kane tilted his hand back and puffed out a perfect smoke ring. "I'll miss you."

*It's just a line,* Miranda told herself as she slammed back into school and trudged down the empty hallway. *He doesn't want you.*

And all her fantasies, all the lies she'd told herself, came crashing down, because that was the truth.

*Play it cool.*

*Play it cool.*

But the halls were empty. There was no one left to appreciate the act. So Miranda dropped it. And, letting out a ragged breath, she finally allowed herself to burst into tears.

*He doesn't want me,* she moaned to herself, chest heaving. She ducked into an empty classroom and closed the door, slumping down to the floor behind it and curling up into a tight ball, rocking back and forth.

She'd always thought that if she could just get him to notice her, just for once get him to see her as an object of desire, that he wouldn't be able to resist.

Well, he'd seen her. He'd gotten the best of her, in every way. He'd hung out with her, he'd flirted with her, he'd kissed her, and after all that?

He'd passed.

It's not that she was invisible.

It's that she was unworthy. Unappealing.

And now she couldn't even retreat into her fantasies, because everything had happened exactly as she'd hoped and it still hadn't been enough.

There was nothing left to hope for.

It was over—and she was done.

# chapter

## 14

Harper stepped up to the podium, and it was so warm and light under the spotlight, all the people beaming up at her with love in their eyes. It was such an amazing view with all the lights and colors and sounds so strange as if she could see them shimmering through the air, glittering filaments streaming toward her ears.

*My turn,* she thought and she took out her speech, but then it seemed so dull and colorless. She was so tired of keeping everything inside tight bottled up pressing against her insides. There was so much pain and now here today she could let it out.

Harper crumpled up her speech and tossed it away. *Thank god for Xanax,* she thought, thinking fondly of the two pills she'd popped before stepping onstage. If she'd been nervous before she now knew that was silly, ridiculous, there was no reason to worry, she was warm, she was loved, this was her moment, and she began to speak.

"I don't know you," she said, sweeping her arms out at

the sea of people. "I know you, and I know you"—she pointed—"but not all of you, and you don't know me. You think you know me, but not the me inside, you know? Not Harper Grace. Who am I? It's like . . ." Train of thought vanished, because there was his face, glowing golden in the middle of the room. "*He* knows me. He loves me, but he won't admit it. He thinks he hates me. But you can't hate me, Adam, because you need me, we're like one person, you and me, together. Remember when we were together for the first time?" She sighed and ran her hands up and down her body and moaned because for a second it was like his hands were her hands, no, like her hands were his hands—whatever it was, it was better than being alone, which is all she ever was anymore, and some-one was trying to make her shut up to go away but she pushed him away and kept talking because she'd been silent for so long. "You couldn't and then you could, and we screwed and—and then you left me all alone. Why would you do that, Adam? Why would you leave me when you said you'd never leave me? I'm so sorry, I'm sorry for everything and everyone and I was just so scared to say it, but I'm weak, I'm weak and bad terrible evil I know, but you said *forever,* Adam. Why would you do that to me? Why would you lie?"

And the principal was pulling at her dragging her away and she gripped the podium because it was too important, she needed an answer, but she'd lost sight of his golden face and now there were only strangers, and their laughter looked black and felt like knives, and then Harper, who had been feeling no pain suddenly felt it all and she broke from the principal's arms.

*Get away,* that was all she could think, all she could do. Must get away.

Adam slumped down in his seat, jaw wide open, eyes squeezed shut. Whatever she was on—and it must have been something—she'd humiliated herself. Not to mention him. He couldn't stand to watch. And it just kept going, forever. *When will they drag her away?* he kept thinking as the horror stretched on, and on. *When will they make her stop?*

Now she was gone, and they were all staring at him instead. He was a part of this freak show, like it or not, and he hated her for dragging him down with her.

And yet—inside, his stomach twisted into a tight, painful knot at the thought of her up there, broken, for all to see.

*Did I do that to her?* he wondered.

And he couldn't help but care.

Maybe she really did love him, in her twisted, fucked-up way. They had dragged her off the podium as she flailed about like an animal—and wouldn't stop screaming his name.

He should go to her. But then everyone would see him get up, walk out, and everyone would know he was a part of this. After all she'd done to him, he was supposed to forgive and forget, just because she had a public meltdown?

For all he knew, this was just another strategy to win him over, and playing into it would just make him look like an idiot, again.

Yes. No. Stay. Go. He froze up.

And by the time he finally made his choice, it was too late. She was gone.

If only life were TiVo'd, and she could rewatch the moment again and again.

*I did that,* she thought, watching Harper flee the stage, not sure whether she felt triumph or nausea. *I won.*

Of course, Harper could never know what Beth had slipped into her drink, or that she'd finally been bested by the one on whom she'd looked down the most. But it hardly mattered—after that performance, Beth suspected it would be a long time before Harper was able to look down at anyone.

Beth had expected it to feel better, sweeter. But all she felt was a sense of finality, as if this had ended things, with a fittingly sordid coup de grâce.

As she'd watched Harper self-destruct, her anger toward Kane and Adam had fallen away. As Harper ranted, and the laughter of the crowd grew louder and crueler, Beth decided that this was it.

She'd taken her revenge—and it had been necessarily brutal, but now it was over.

This is what they called "closure," she supposed. It was a good word, because the past few months now felt like a tedious story she'd plowed through, pitting herself against the pages that mounted up with no end in sight. She'd made it through, and now she would shut the book forever. She would throw it away.

Beth was different now—thanks, she supposed, to Harper, to all of them. She was stronger. Harder.

There were four months to graduation, and she would spend them alone and miserable. But she would deal. She had let Harper turn her into the kind of person she'd always despised, and maybe there was no going back from that. But she could go forward.

Kaia made her decision. She would call the police, tell her story, take responsibility. She was in the right, after all. She was no criminal, and no victim, either. She had just done what had to be done, and that's just what she would do now. Not because it was what her parents would have wanted, or what a million Lifetime movies would have advised, but because she just knew it was the right thing. She'd let Powell make her feel weak—but now that was over, and this was the way to be strong.

And then Harper ran out of the school, past a smirking Kane, past a zoned-out Secret Service guy, across the parking lot, and straight toward Kaia. It was like a sign.

Harper stopped a few feet away, her breath ragged, tears streaming down her face. "Kaia?"

"What's going on? What's wrong?"

"I don't—" She furiously rubbed at one of her eyes, her hand curled into a fist and tucked into the cuff of her sleeve. "Nothing. It's fine. Nothing. Let's just go, okay?" she said, her face lighting up like a child's.

"Go where?"

"Away. Just away." Obviously upset, the words were spilling out of her almost too quickly to follow, but they made sense. "Like you said before, let's be gone. Jump into your car. Go. Out."

Kaia didn't stop to think. Get away, just drive—not forever, not for more than a few hours, but it would be enough. She could clear her head, gather her strength, and prepare for the coming storm. It was just what she needed;

given Harper's unexplained meltdown, just what they both needed. And when they came back, she would go to the cops, she promised herself. She would take care of everything.

Harper grabbed the keys from Kaia's hand and jumped into the front seat. "Where to?" she asked. "We can go anywhere, I just want to feel the road beneath me—you know, drive and drive until it's all behind us—"

Kaia opened the passenger door and hopped in, glad not to be stuck behind the wheel, so she could just relax, watch the world stream by through the window, lose her focus, and let all her worries escape. "Anywhere," she agreed. "I don't care. Let's just go."

She'd barely gotten the door closed when Harper shifted the car into gear and peeled out of the lot, pulling a sharp U-turn and speeding down the road, heading out of town.

"Harper, slow down!" Kaia gripped the dashboard as they flew over a speed bump.

"I can never go back there," Harper was saying, pushing the car faster and faster. They whipped around a sharp curve and Kaia gasped—but at least now they'd passed through the town limits and were out in the open, where speed was exhilarating, not deadly.

Kaia's apprehension mixed with her stress and exhaustion, and through a strange alchemy, she suddenly found herself smiling, pressing the button to lower the top on the car. Suddenly, the speed *was* exhilarating. Like a roller coaster. And just as she used to do before she got too old for such things, Kaia raised her arms and screamed into the wind.

"We're getting out!" Harper cried, and Kaia closed her eyes, letting the wind thunder in her ears, the sun warm her face. Whatever had happened, whatever would happen, they had this one moment.

And in this moment, they were finally free.

He didn't see them until it was too late.

They came barreling over the hill out of nowhere, swerving from lane to lane as if they owned the road. He'd been up all night, driving across the state. His reflexes maybe weren't what they should have been, and the van was hard to maneuver.

He veered out of the way as soon as he spotted them— but it wasn't soon enough.

The scream of the metal as his van sliced through the body of their car—it was a sound he'd remember for the rest of his life.

It was a long, slow, grinding whine, a high screech, a sickening crunch.

The van was big, tough. And when it was over, the van was pretty much intact.

The BMW wasn't as lucky. The force of the impact had knocked it off the road, flipped it over, crushed it.

It barely looked like a car anymore. And whoever had been inside—

He looked away.

*Not my fault,* he assured himself. *Not my problem.*

The van was dented, but still running. And he had a long drive ahead of him. Better to start now.

Someone else would come along, eventually.

They always did.

It hurt to open her eyes. It hurt to move.

She did neither.

There may have been sirens, in the distance. Or maybe it was just the loud whine in her head. Or maybe she was screaming. Still screaming. She remembered—

What?

Horns.

Squeals.

And then she had been weightless, flying.

Darkness.

She could hear her breathing, ragged and slow. And she could feel pain. Everywhere.

*Alive,* she decided. *I hurt, therefore I am.*

There was something missing, though.

She could hear her breathing—but nothing else.

She remembered her screams—but nothing else.

She opened her eyes. All she saw, at first, was the bright white blazing sky. Then, slowly: tangled metal. Smoke. Licks of flame. Dirt. Rivers of red. And . . .

A body. Still.

She tried to open her mouth and call out. But no sound came. And in the wreckage, nothing—no one—moved.

She tried to reach out, to crawl over, but she was swept up in a wave of pain. It sucked her down, deep, back into the darkness, and she closed her eyes again, and let it drag her under.

Help was on the way.

And, eventually, it showed up.

Two ambulances tore off toward town, one speeding

down the highway, lights blazing, sirens blaring. The other took its time, stopped at traffic lights, observed the speed limit. Its lights were dark, its sirens silent.

There was no hurry.

There was no one left to save.

# Sloth

"Where to?"

Beth leaned her head back against the seat and half-heartedly tried to wipe some of the grime off her window, as if the answer to his question might arise from a better view. "Wherever." The word came out as a sigh, fading to silence before the last syllable.

"Okay." Reed drove in circles for a while. He had nowhere to be. When she'd called, he had been at his father's garage, tinkering with an exhaust system and ready for a break. "Can you come?" she'd asked. And for whatever reason, he'd dropped everything and hopped in the truck. He'd found her slouched at the foot of a tree, just in front of the school, hugging her arms to her chest and shivering. She wouldn't tell him anything, but when he extended a hand to help her into the truck, she squeezed.

It's not like they were friends, he told himself. But she needed something, and he had nothing better to do. He couldn't help but notice that she relaxed into her seat, stretching out along the cracked vinyl, unlike Kaia, who almost always perched on the edge and sat poker-straight in an effort to have as little contact with the "filthy" interior as possible. Beth also hadn't commented on his torn overalls or the smudges of grease splashed across his face and blackening his fingers.

Reed caught himself and for a moment felt the urge to stop the car and toss her out on the side of the road. But it passed.

"Wanna talk about it?" he asked.

She shook her head. "I don't even want to *think* about it," she said. "Any chance you can take me somewhere where I can do that? Stop thinking?"

She said it bitterly, as if it were an impossible challenge. But she obviously didn't know who she was dealing with.

Reed swung the car around the empty road in a sharp U-turn and pressed down on the gas pedal. She sighed again heavily, and without thinking, he reached over to put a hand on her shoulder, but stopped in midair—maybe because Kaia had trained him well: no greasy fingers on white shirts. Or maybe because he didn't want to touch her.

He put his hand back on the wheel and began drumming out a light, simple beat. "I know just the place," he assured her. "We'll be there soon." It felt good to have a destination.

Miranda suddenly felt completely sober and clear. But she couldn't have been, or she wouldn't have stood up and walked purposefully off toward the crop of Joshua trees, where she'd seen half the basketball team breaking bottles and doing keg stands. If she wasn't drunk, where did she get the nerve to wrap her arms around Adam and whisper in his ear? "I need you, now."

She didn't think about the consequences or fear humiliation. She just acted, tugging him away from the group, deeper into the trees. She didn't need to think. She'd come to this party to give in to her desires. At the time, those had been: longing, lust, hope.

Now they'd been replaced with one: revenge. She didn't pause to acknowledge that to herself or explain it to Adam. She didn't even need to take a deep breath before kissing him. And she had to admit that Harper had been right. The chiseled face and perfect body were a definite turn-on.

"Miranda?" Adam was out of it, completely, his face slack and his words thick. "Whuh?"

"This doesn't have to mean anything," she said, stripping off her shirt. "It's just for fun." She tugged at the edge of his shirt, and stumbled against him. "It's a party, right?"

Adam didn't say anything. But he let her tug him down to the ground, and he didn't resist as she ran her fingers through his hair. She didn't know how to seduce someone, or how to follow up the first move with a second one. *Harper* would have known.

She lay down on her side, ignored the sharp edges digging into her. "Come here," she told Adam, hooking her finger into his collar and jerking him toward her. He toppled over with a grunt, then rolled to face her. "Miranda, I'm not really—"

Miranda jerked her face toward his. Their noses bumped, and then awkwardly but without hesitation, their lips met.

His face was stubbly and his hair too short. His breath was sour, his kiss was rough, angry, but at least she had *acted*. And her eyes were dry. He grunted like an animal, and she accidentally bit his tongue, and the rocks beneath them felt like they were drawing blood. But she persevered. She closed her eyes, kissed him harder, and tried not to pretend he was someone else.

"Aw yeah, that's right." The one named Hale clapped his hands together once as Fish hoisted a giant glass tube out of the crawl space behind the lopsided couch. "Give it here, dude."

"Hold your shit," Fish said, flourishing a lighter.

Beth tucked her hair behind her ears and tried not to look nervous.

*Get out,* her instincts screamed.

"You okay?" Reed asked, as if he could sense her discomfort. It probably wasn't too hard, she realized, since she was squeezed into the corner of the couch, as far away from Fish as she could get, her arms scrunched up against her sides and her mouth glued shut. She nodded.

"Over here, baby," Hale requested, beckoning Fish to hand over the bong.

"Dude, don't you have any manners?" Fish grabbed one of the discarded fast-food wrappers off the ground, scrunched it up, and threw it at his head. "Ladies first." He stretched across the couch and handed the long glass tube to Beth, giving her an encouraging nod. She noticed that his hair was even paler than hers, and almost as long.

"Guys, I don't think . . ." Reed, who was perched on an orange milk crate, leaned forward, speaking softly enough that only Beth could hear. "You don't have to. We can go, if you want."

He'd said the same thing when they'd walked into the

house and he'd seen the look on her face. There were some empty rooms upstairs, he'd suggested, if she didn't want to hang with the guys—and then he'd flushed, stumbling over his words, hurrying to explain that he didn't mean *bedrooms*, not like that. Or they could just go. Anywhere. But for some reason, Beth had insisted they stay, and now here she was, the bong delicately balanced in her hands, the nauseating fumes rising toward her, a trippy hip-hop beat shaking the walls—which were covered with fading posters of half-naked women—and for the first time that day, Beth smiled.

"Just tell me what to do," she said firmly. She'd always sworn she wouldn't smoke pot—it was illegal, not to mention dangerous. But she was already a criminal, she reminded herself, and danger didn't scare her anymore— things couldn't get much worse. If she could find a way to turn off her brain, maybe, for a little while, things could actually be better.

Reed didn't try to talk her out of it, and didn't ask about the sudden change of heart. He just rested his hand on top of hers and guided the opening toward her mouth, then put his finger over a small hole and flicked on the lighter. "Take a deep breath, but don't—"

A spasm of coughing racked her body and she inadvertently jerked the bong away, spilling warm, grayish water all over her jeans. "Sorry," she mumbled, her face flushing red.

"No problem. Take a smaller breath the next time," Reed suggested. "Suck it into your mouth and then kind of breathe it down into your lungs."

"Okay, I think—" She broke off as another cough

ripped out of her. Reed put his hand on her back, rubbing in small, slow circles.

"Take it easy," he said quietly. "Go slow."

"I'm okay. I'm okay," she protested, straightening up so that he would take his hand away, even though it was the last thing she wanted. "Let me try this again." This time she got a hot lungful down without much coughing. She passed the bong to Fish and leaned back against the couch, waiting for it to take effect.

"Man, this is some good shit!" Fish sputtered as he took his mouth off the tube.

"Totally," Hale agreed after his turn, already looking tuned out to the world.

Reed didn't say anything after his turn, just fixed his eyes on Beth. She looked away, waiting for the room to start spinning or her tongue to start feeling absurdly big. She felt nothing, except the same panic and fear she'd felt for days.

"Time for another little toke," Hale said eagerly, grabbing it back. "Yeah, that's good. Dude, I'm totally high."

"It's like . . . yeah. Cool," Fish agreed.

"Hey, uh . . . Reed's girl, you feeling it?" Hale asked.

Lesson one of getting stoned: Talk about how stoned you are. Beth learned fast. "Yeah," she lied. "It's really wild."

"Dude, Fish, you know what I just realized? You totally look like a girl," Hale cried, a burst of giggles flooding out of him.

Fish ran his fingers through his straggly, straw-colored hair as if realizing for the first time it was there, then looked at Beth in wonderment. "Yeah," he agreed. "I must be hot. Blonds are *hot*."

Beth laughed weakly and searched herself for hysteria,

paranoia, munchies, *something* to testify to the fact that she'd just ingested an illegal substance for the first time in her life. But she felt, if anything, more self-conscious than ever, as if they could all tell that her mind was running at normal speed and that she was, even here, a total fraud.

"You usually don't feel much the first time," Reed confided, again using that just-for-her voice. "You didn't do it wrong."

Once again, he'd known exactly what she was thinking. A horrifying thought occurred to her: What if he really could tell what she was thinking? What if he knew about Harper, and about Kaia, about everything? And even if he didn't, what would happen if he found out?

*Maybe this is paranoia,* Beth thought, and now a hysterical giggle did escape her. *Maybe I am high.*

"So, you guys, like, live here?" she asked, trying to make her voice sound as slow and foggy as theirs.

"Fish and Hale do," Reed explained. "And I crash here sometimes."

"He brings his *ladies* here," Hale cackled. "All except—"

"Dude, shut up," Fish snapped, pelting him with another fast-food wrapper—this one seemed to have a chunk of something oozing out of it.

"Oh yeah. Right. Sorry, bro. Didn't mean to—"

"Whatever." Reed turned the stereo up and then threw himself down on the couch in between Beth and Fish. He leaned his head back, closed his eyes, and kicked his legs up on the milk crate. "Awesome song," he sighed.

*When in Rome . . . ,* Beth thought, *do as the potheads do.* She closed her eyes, kicked her feet up on the same milk crate, so that one leg crossed over Reed's, and forced a serene smile. "I'm, uh, totally hungry," she said tentatively. "Anyone got anything to eat?"

"Uhhhhhhhhhhhhhh." Miranda opened her eyes, squinting in the blinding light of morning. She twisted her head to the left but stopped, abruptly, as a wave of nausea swept over her. Better not to move, she decided. Her head felt like a bowling ball and her mouth was so dry she feared that if she started to talk, it might crack open. Good thing she had no intention of talking. The sound of her breathing was thunder enough.

She felt like her brain and body weren't quite attached, and that if she moved the latter, she might break the former. So she lay still. She focused on taking one breath, then another. She tried to ignore the throbbing pain in her head. Maybe in a few minutes she'd have the strength to get up and brush her teeth, which felt like they were covered in steel wool. As for breakfast . . . the thought made her gag. What if her mother—

And only then did she realize. She wasn't in her bedroom, or in a bed. *Go slow,* she warned herself as a flood of confusion threatened to drown her. *Take stock:*

Arms and legs—fully functional, if too heavy to move.

Location—the sun was killing her, jagged ground dug into her. So, outside. Somewhere, for some reason.

Miscellaneous—her shirt was off. Her left arm was squashed between her chest and the ground, but her right arm was propped up on something. It moved, gently rising and falling, and she realized her breaths weren't the only ones she heard. Groaning, she twisted her head around.

"Ooooooooooooh noooooooooo." The words came out in

a weak and scratchy wheeze, but they were loud enough. He opened his eyes.

"Unnnh?" Adam shook his head and propped himself up, then, thinking better of it, dropped back down to the ground. "What am I . . . what are you . . . ?"

*There was a party,* Miranda remembered. The images were floating lazily around her brain and she tried to snatch them and put them into some kind of order.

*Beer. Lots of beer.*

*Kane's arms holding her up.*

*More beer.*

*The trees. Adam. Unbuttoning her shirt. His tongue . . .*

"What did I do?" she whispered, her throat burning with the effort. "Adam," she croaked. His eyes had slipped shut again. His chest was bare. "Adam!" she said louder, with more energy than she had.

"Uh?"

She realized her arm was still lying on top of him. She pulled it away, lurching over onto her back. The sun was so horribly bright. "Do you remember what . . . what did we . . ." She was almost afraid to ask. "Did we . . . ?"

Beth drew in a breath and tried not to cough out the smoke. "This is harder than it looks," she sputtered, lying back against the sleeping bag.

"You get the hang of it," Reed assured her. He lay down next to her, and for a long time, all she could hear was their breathing, and the whistling of the wind. "You feeling anything?" he asked.

"I don't know. . . ." The words sounded strange, and *felt* strange, as if her tongue had suddenly doubled in size. She stuck it out at him. "Does my tongue look weird?" (This came out sounding more like "Doz ba tog look eered?") She burst into giggles before he could answer.

"Yeah, you're feeling it," he said, satisfied.

Beth waved her hand in front of her face, marveling at the fact that it was too dark to see. *Maybe I don't have a hand anymore,* she thought. *Maybe I'm just a mind.* The theory seemed startlingly profound, and she was about to explain it to Reed, but the words slipped away from her.

"I never knew why she was with me, you know?" His words seemed like they were dropping out of the sky, unconnected to either of them. "I mean, I'm . . . and she was . . . yeah. Like the way she talked. It was like everything she said came out of a book. Like . . ."

Beth zoned out, just listening to the pleasant rise and fall of his voice, tuning for scattered words and phrases— "never again," "in the water," "can't stop," "sundress," "going crazy," and, several times, "why"—but she couldn't focus enough to draw them together into a single thread. Every time she tried, she would realize that the ground was hard and soft at the same time, or the air tasted like peppermint, and she would wander off into her head.

The world seemed so huge, and so small at the same time, like she and Reed were the only things in existence. And wouldn't everything be so much easier if that were true. The world felt fresh. The sharp wind against her face, the rough polyester beneath her. Reed's hand brushing, just slightly, against hers—she'd never felt so *there.*

"Are you happy?" she asked.

"No. You?"

"No. But—" She searched for the words that described

how she *did* feel, a certainty that she'd never be happy combined with a strange acceptance and even contentment, as if she were floating along and the current was strong but she could trust where it would take her, so she could just close her eyes, sink back, and relax. She felt like she understood everything at once, with a deep clarity— but when she tried to name it, assign words and sentences to the certainty, it flowed away. The closer she drew, the blurrier it got. So she gave up. "But it's okay," she concluded simply.

She heard Reed take a sharp, deep breath and let it out slowly. "Yeah. It's okay."

# about the author

Robin Wasserman enjoys writing about high school—but wakes up every day grateful that she doesn't have to relive it. She recently abandoned the beaches and boulevards of Los Angeles for the chilly embrace of the East Coast, as all that sun and fun gave her too little to complain about. She now lives and writes in New York City, which she claims to love for its vibrant culture and intellectual life. In reality, she doesn't make it to museums nearly enough, and actually just loves the city for its pizza, its shopping, and the fact that at 3 a.m. you can always get anything you need—and you can get it delivered.

As many as 1 in 3 Americans
who have HIV... don't know it.

**TAKE CONTROL.**
**KNOW YOUR STATUS.**
**GET TESTED.**

To learn more about HIV testing,
or get a free guide to HIV and
other sexually transmitted diseases:

**www.knowhivaids.org**
**1-866-344-KNOW**